EYE
OF THE
PEACOCK

ROBERTA WORTHINGTON

Tannhauser Press, Fredericksburg, VA

ISBN: 13:978-1-945994-28-9
ISBN: 10:1-945994-28-2

Printed by Tannhauser Press, Fredericksburg VA

Cover design by Aaron La Porta www.wordsandnames.com

The text for this book is set in Times New Roman. Chapter headings are set in Matura MT Script Capitals.

To those we have known before.

EYE OF THE
PEACOCK

One

THE TOE OF Aubrey's sneaker caught on the threshold. Her knees made contact with the floor first, and her palms slapped the polished wood as she sprawled into the room. Her spiral notebook, which she had hoped would make her appear organized, twirl-slid out of her grasp and away. On any other day – and it happened practically every day – she would have been embarrassed, but she was too awe struck. She physically worked to shut her jaw so she didn't look even more ridiculous as she gawked up and around at the room. Light fought its way through three-story windows covering one wall of the venerable room, but the archaic trappings seemed to be winning. Dark leather benches, an overpowering fireplace carved from a slab of stone, and taxidermy that gazed passively from every wall and shelf, gave the place a dim feeling.

"You okay?" A voice spoke out of the gloom. As the owner of the voice emerged from the shadows, Aubrey's imagination warped him into a caricature of a bowling pin with a mop of blonde curls on his head. The thought made her crack a smile.

If he would just realize that the red polo did nothing to help his physique, she thought.

He handed Aubrey back her notebook. Girls didn't normally fall at his feet – literally or otherwise. In the place where he felt most comfortable, suddenly he felt his usual awkward self.

"It's like a castle in here," Aubrey said trying to regain her composure. She pushed herself up, stood and dusted off her knees. Her eyes turned to the second floor where a hallway of mahogany arches and railings ringed three sides of the room like a balcony. A bear skin rested its head on the railing closest to the fireplace chimney.

"Just this room really," the young man said, gaining confidence with the familiar. "It was modeled after a castle keep's main hall. The rest is more like a house." He chuckled a little. "A big house, but a house. Are you the new docent?"

"Yeah, I suppose so," Aubrey replied still trying to mentally catch herself.

A month ago, in May, her guidance counselor, Mr. Matthews, told her she was going to have to start community service in earnest if she intended to stay in the National Honor Society and start applying to colleges.

"Your grades are pretty good, especially science,"

Mr. Matthews had said.

She had to agree. Earth Science was okay this year. She enjoyed Mrs. Davidson's class. During one lesson, Mrs. Davidson had stopped everything when she saw a storm brewing outside. She told the students to turn their desks around to face the windows, which she proceeded to open. She had instructed them that instead of screaming as their papers flew off their desks, to use all their senses to observe what was happening around them. They shivered as they were blown upon, and rain whipped their faces. They wrote furiously as the storm raged around them. Afterwards, they discussed their notes and discovered how weather fronts worked. It was a lesson Aubrey would never forget.

Yes, science came easy to her, but having Mrs. Davidson for a teacher helped. She was the kind of teacher who cared about her students' learning. She had even given each of them a copy of the periodic table of elements – something they wouldn't really use until next year's chemistry class, but she wanted them to see how all of the elements came from the environment, how the two classes were connected. Aubrey was intrigued by the diagram of lettered building blocks, and in her free time she had researched several of the symbols on the internet and tried to unlock their mystery.

"But you need to be well-rounded if you intend to be competitive with colleges," Mr. Matthews had droned on during their session. "Volunteer work will help with that."

Aubrey had sat in the uncomfortable wooden chair in

Mr. Matthews' office, the heels of her canvas sneakers pulled up against the front legs of the chair so her binders and text books would stay piled on her knees. She didn't like being called into Mr. Matthews' office. He normally only saw kids who were in trouble or had emotional dilemmas. She had tried hard to avoid his notice. Aubrey tried hard to avoid everyone's notice. But this community service thing had caught up with her.

She had peered out from behind her long, dark, crimson-tipped hair and scanned the list of possibilities Mr. Matthews had shoved across his desk at her. Aubrey felt herself growing more and more dejected. She hated the smell of old people, and she was allergic to animals. That didn't leave many options. But there was one, a docent at an estate. As Mr. Matthews had explained it to her, she had realized that it vaguely had to do with history. She was also enjoying Ms. Widman's history class this year – the way she told stories instead of just giving notes. Maybe that one would work. So Aubrey had chosen it, not really because she understood what her responsibilities would be or what she would need to do, but as a last resort.

This morning, under a gleaming sun and temperatures already in the 70s, she slammed the passenger door of her friend Pitch's car in the parking lot of the Fairview estate. Most people tried to avoid Pitch with his black jeans, Goth t-shirts, and dyed black hair. But Aubrey had known Oliver Pitcher since kindergarten, and when they entered high school two years ago, they became recluses together. Recently, though, things had become strained.

At lunch last week, she caught him looking at her oddly.

"You okay?" she had asked at the time. "We still friends?"

"Sure," he had said with a finality that didn't sound all that comforting.

Now, closing the door of his Ford Pinto, Aubrey leaned down to the open passenger window. "Thanks Pitch," she said, but she was left standing there, gravel spraying from his rear tires. That wasn't like him. He couldn't be upset with her, or he wouldn't have agreed to drop her off for her first day at Fairview. He knew she was desperate for a lift after yet another argument with her mother had eliminated that ride. Maybe he was just late for his job walking Mrs. Wilson's Pekinese or Miss Richardson's Cockapoodle – another part of Pitch that people wouldn't have expected, but to which she was privy.

She pushed her confusion about Pitch from her mind and focused on the blond boy in front of her. Now she was the new docent, whatever that meant.

"I'm Gerard," said the boy in the red polo.

"I'm Aubrey. Are you going to train me?"

"No Audrey..."

She cut him off, eternally annoyed. "It's Au-brey," she said, enunciating the middle of her name. Other than her clumsiness, it was the other guaranteed thing about her. People were going to screw up her name.

"Oh sorry. No. That's old Ida's job."

She rolled her eyes. No, not an old person. She hated

old people.

"There's a lot to learn. Ida will give you a notebook to study." Gerard rambled on as Aubrey followed him out of the castle room and down the main hallway of the house. She found it difficult to look at everything and listen to Gerard at the same time. She was not usually this overwhelmed by new surroundings, but this place... this place was awesome in the truest sense of the word.

"At first, you'll probably shadow Ida on her tours. That's what I did," Gerard rattled on casually as he led the way. "And then she makes you take her on a tour. If she thinks you've got enough facts down, you'll team for a while, you leading the tour and her piping in or fielding the questions. If you're a quick study you'll be on your own in two weeks."

"Have you worked here long?" Aubrey asked as she trotted along behind him.

Gerard smiled over his shoulder at her. "Sometimes it feels like forever!" He stopped briefly to straighten a picture on the wall. "There are times it just seems like I belong here."

Aubrey's mouth pulled sideways in a quirky smile. Fairview was so ornate, it was difficult to imagine anyone belonging here. Her curiosity began to override the idea that this position was solely for school credit.

Aubrey paid more attention on their short walk than she was used to giving anything. Everyday household items and decorations filled tabletops and walls. Pushing her dark hair out of her eyes, she tried to peek into rooms, to soak it all in. But somehow she still got turned around.

Judging by the formal furnishings, she and Gerard had ended up in a parlor of sorts. There was a round alcove to one side furnished with an intricately painted porcelain garden table and four matching stools. She wandered over, but not to admire the exquisite green, yellow and blue pattern of the Chinese antique. Instead, Aubrey reached out a hand to pet an equally extraordinary stuffed white peacock perched on the table, its tail feathers forever sculpted to gently flow over the table's edge.

"Don't touch that!"

Gerard's voice jarred her, but his admonition came at the exact moment Aubrey swore she saw the peacock swivel its eye toward her and blink.

Two

STARTLED ON two fronts, Aubrey jerked her hand away from the taxidermied bird and turned back to Gerard, shock resonating in her eyes. Just then, an elderly woman entered the room.

"Ida, this is Aubrey. Aubrey, Ida. She's our head docent here at Fairview." Gerard's voice was polite again, no doubt for the elderly woman's benefit.

"It's so nice to meet you Audrey," Ida chirped.

"Au-brey," Aubrey automatically corrected as she gave the bird a second glance, but Ida didn't seem to notice.

"It's good to meet you, too." Aubrey shook Ida's cold, arthritic hand. Ida's grey hair was cut in a short, stylish bob with wispy bangs over her wrinkled forehead. Old age had shrunk her to about four-foot-seven, and Aubrey gratefully noticed she smelled of Channel No. 5. The woman was wearing a red shirt that matched Gerard's.

"I take it Gerard has filled you in a little. Let's step out onto the porch to talk. It's such a lovely spring day. Do you like iced tea?"

"Yes, I do," Aubrey replied, as she followed Ida's self-assured steps out one room and into another where Ida stopped to pick up a pile of papers. Ida then led them through a wooden screen door that slammed behind them. They stepped onto a generous, curved veranda set with several wicker tables and chairs as if it were a café. Gerard settled at one of the tables.

"I'm glad you volunteered to help us, Audrey –"

Aubrey opened her mouth to correct Ida again, but thought better of it. She, too, attempted to settle herself at the table, although her foot caught on the leg of the chair, and she stumbled a little. She didn't think Ida or Gerard noticed.

"Fairview benefits from all the volunteers who now help keep it running. It is a treasure we cannot afford to lose. You're a member of the team now," Ida said, smiling and handing Aubrey a red polo shirt. "Starting any new job is overwhelming. Prepare yourself! Here's a map of Fairview, another map of the grounds and gardens, the basic script for tours, and this book to read for a pretty complete history of Fairview." She piled them one after the next on the table as she announced their contents. "That's your homework for tomorrow."

"And you'll have to do something with that hair," Gerard chimed in.

Aubrey wrinkled her nose. No one told her what to do with her hair. "Are hair styles part of the dress code?"

"That's not what I mean," he said. "Just that that crimson is going to clash with the shirt."

Aubrey stared at Gerard not knowing if he was joking or not. Ida filled the awkward silence.

"There's a tour starting in a couple of minutes. Why don't you come along with me, and then Gerard can take you on a tour of the grounds."

Ida, who hadn't sat down to rest, took a sip of her iced tea. She looked ready to leave to meet the tour group, but glancing around, Aubrey couldn't spot anyone. She pushed her chair away from the table. She intended to follow Ida, but instead was drawn to the stone railing of the porch. Without realizing she had taken the steps, Aubrey found herself leaning on the railing soaking in the view as if her life depended on it.

"Quite breathtaking, isn't it?" Ida said, pride beaming on her face.

"Is my mouth still hanging open?" Aubrey asked, pulling her gaze from a vast, formal Italian garden that spread from the veranda like an Oriental carpet. She smiled sheepishly, trying to hide her embarrassment. But she couldn't look away for long. The garden, she noticed, was divided into quadrants by a generously wide walkway, which intersected in the center at a three-tiered fountain. Each quadrant was sunk several feet below the walkway, so passersby could appreciate the fleur-de-lis pattern played out in red and yellow coleus on a green canvas. Low boxwood shrubs outlined the quadrants, and on each corner, urns with pointed boxwoods stood sentinel. A row of cedars provided a backdrop on the horizon. But the person who designed the garden had cleverly intertwined architecture with manipulated nature. In the far left corner, Romanesque marble columns supported the domed iron grillwork of a garden house. A lengthy, pillared pergola draped with vines bordered the entire right side of the view. It was waiting for a summer evening stroll.

"It's just that I've never seen something so…. Well, I just can't believe I've lived here all my life and never realized this place was here."

"Well, I hear that people who live near Niagara Falls don't go to see it either!" Ida mused. Gerard chuckled as if he knew he should.

As her eyes poured over every detail of the intricate floral display, Aubrey saw someone standing in her peripheral vision just behind her right shoulder. For a split second she assumed it was Ida, or even Gerard, come to share the view. But then she realized it was a girl wearing white. When she turned to look at her, the girl was gone. Aubrey closed her eyes and gave her head a quick shake. As she opened her eyes, at the left edge of her vision, she saw another figure – a man in a tweed jacket – fleeing across the lawn adjacent to the formal garden. Oddly, when she turned to get a better look, her eyes squinted in confusion, he too was gone.

"Let's go, Audrey," Ida chirped again. "People are depending on us!"

Three

AUBREY STOOD with Ida in their matching red polos near the main staircase of Fairview. At Ida's gentle suggestion, Aubrey had twisted her dark hair into a bun to hide the crimson tips. A group of a dozen tourists, mostly senior citizens, were clustered around them. Before stepping foot in Fairview, Aubrey had never seen a staircase this wide. It was at least twice as wide as a normal staircase. It reached a landing where Aubrey thought a floor should be, then turned and ascended another flight to the second floor. At the landing, light flooded through the gemstone colors of a magnificent stained glass window depicting two peacocks sitting among the green leaves of a tree. One peacock was the typical blue and the other a spectral white. Their tail feathers cascaded from the branch. The image made Aubrey recall the stuffed peacock she had seen a few minutes earlier, but Ida's words interrupted the thought.

"Now we'll go upstairs to tour the bedrooms," Ida announced. She led the group to the landing, which was bathed in sunlight shining through the enormous stained glass window. Aubrey brought up the rear and any stragglers. There were "oohs" and "aahs" over the craftsmanship of the colored glass, but Ida was quick to point out the less obvious.

"Make sure you note the family photos on the table," she said. She gestured to several as she spoke. "Claire Somerton and her husband, Edgar, are featured here. Mrs. Somerton's sister, Gladys, and her two children, who often spent portions of the summer with the family, are here. And the close-up on the right is of the couple's daughter Maeve. We'll see Maeve's bedroom first. When we get there you can go in and look around for yourselves. Please remember not to sit on any of the furniture."

Ida led them up the remainder of the stairs and to a bedroom across the hall. The room displayed a bed, and beyond it, a sitting area with an overstuffed chair, footstool, and a lady's writing desk. The room was well lit from generous windows in the sitting area. Ida pointed out, through a doorway to the right, a bathroom with running water, and to the left, a doorway that led to a Juliet balcony overlooking the Great Hall hung with taxidermy. Aubrey slid along the side of the group, inconspicuously working her way toward the windows so that she could bring up the rear of the group again as Ida had instructed her to do. It was a tricky maneuver, but Aubrey was slowly realizing she wanted to make a good impression with Ida. She was trying diligently to absorb as much as she could of what Ida was saying, but couldn't help feeling her mind drift. At school, she normally tried hard *not* to be noticed. She wondered if she could lead a tour as Ida was now doing. Standing near the bathroom, Aubrey realized that members of the group had begun asking questions.

"Did the house have running water when they lived here?" one man asked, unbelieving.

"It did," Ida said. "It seems unusual, but they were very rich, and the system used gravity to pull the water through from a cistern on the roof."

"This balcony is beautiful," one woman said. "What a lovely room for a young girl."

"Did she inherit the estate?" another woman asked.

"Unfortunately, Maeve died when she was seventeen." There was a collective gasp from the crowd.

"What did she die of?" one man asked.

"Reports are sketchy. Most say it must have been a heart attack. The story goes that she ate dinner with her mother on the veranda that afternoon. She felt sick afterward, collapsed, and died right there on the spot. Terribly unusual, but people think there must have been an obscure heart issue in the family."

As Aubrey flicked back a crimson-tipped swatch of hair that had gone astray, she registered the surprised and saddened faces of the elderly around her, obviously upset by a life ended too soon. She was glancing at an elderly man when a younger face over his shoulder caught her eye. There were no young people in the group. Then she realized the face she saw, blonde and blue-eyed, came from the mirror in the nearby washroom.

"I hate to be melodramatic," said one woman with red-rimmed glasses, a paisley jacket and a blue rinse on her hair, "but is Fairview haunted?" Aubrey's eyes flicked to the woman with the well-timed question.

"You know," Ida said, leaning in and dropping her voice conspiratorially, "I've always thought so." She straightened again. "How could anyone leave a place so beautiful?" She gave a light laugh, and her eyes twinkled mischievously.

"But has anyone ever seen or heard any ghosts?" the woman pressed seriously. Aubrey's eyes flicked back to the bathroom mirror. It was empty. She realized her heart was thumping.

"I must say I've felt their spirits here," Ida said confidently. "Sometimes when you walk into a room you feel like someone walked around the corner just ahead of you." The woman nodded her head in satisfaction.

The tour continued through the house for another twenty minutes or so, and Ida led the group back to the home's main entrance near the Great Hall where Gerard was ready with a small tram to take the seniors on a tour of the grounds.

When the last senior was loaded onto the tram, Ida turned back to the door and Aubrey.

"Ida?" Aubrey stopped her. "You know what you were saying upstairs about Fairview being haunted?"

"Oh, honey!" Ida patted her on the shoulder as she

headed inside. "Fairview isn't haunted! I just say those things to spice it up a bit!"

"It was a lie?"

Ida turned back to Aubrey, and her smile fell. "I don't think of it as a lie," she said. "That woman would have been so disappointed if there hadn't been any ghosts – I could tell. I gave her just enough to stir her imagination. I didn't invent any stories."

"I suppose so," Aubrey said, staring at the worn cobblestones and remembering the face in the mirror.

four

"GERARD, now that you're back, could you give Aubrey a general overview?"

"Will do, Ida." He downed the end of his iced tea.

"An overview?" Aubrey's head was already spinning with information about Fairview. She didn't know if she could retain any more.

"Yeah, c'mon. Leave your stuff, but bring the map of the grounds," Gerard advised, as he trotted down a short flight of stone steps from the porch toward the lawn where Aubrey thought she had seen the fleeing man in the tweed coat.

Gerard and Aubrey walked along the side of the house until they reached the other end of the mansion and what looked like a generous, pillared carport. The driveway curved under it and continued in a northerly direction, but Gerard headed in the opposite direction away from the house. Aubrey followed him a short distance to a large grey outbuilding with five pale yellow barn doors across its front. Outside were parked several golf carts. Gerard wedged himself into the seat behind the wheel and started the engine. His confidence sputtered as he watched Aubrey's willowy form jog around the opposite side of the golf cart. Aubrey grabbed the upright that supported the vehicle's roof and swung herself into the passenger seat. She nearly missed. He didn't mind her clumsiness. And even with that crimson hair, she was quite pretty, he thought.

"We might as well start at the beginning," Gerard said, pulling his job into focus. He turned the golf cart around and headed toward the front of the estate without saying another word. Aubrey realized they were backtracking toward the parking lot where Pitch had dropped her off, but Gerard passed the parking lot and a sprawling greenhouse complex with a domed palm house at its center. The massive, arched, wrought iron gates came into view.

"The main gates weren't always attached to a stone wall." Gerard blurted the seemingly random fact out of nowhere. "Originally there was a hedge, but Claire Somerton replaced it with this stone wall in 1902. It took 1,500 men five years to build the wall."

"For privacy?" Aubrey reasoned.

"Oddly enough, yes. But then Mrs. Somerton opened the grounds to the public once a week on Sundays for several hours."

"That was generous," she noted.

"Yeah. The people in town would come in for walks

and picnics. Even just to see the deer."

"Deer?"

"She bought a herd of deer for the west side of the property." Gerard turned his head, grinning at her, and once again, Aubrey could not be sure if he was joking with her.

"You've got to be kidding." The doubt burst from her. He *had* to be joking.

"Nope. Where's your map?" She spread it across her leg, flattening out the folds with her hand. "Right here." He pointed to an area far from where they were. For a fleeting instant Aubrey noticed his hands. They were strong hands, she thought. Oddly strong, as if they did a lot of manual labor. It was a pity the rest of him was rather…well, awkward.

Gerard stopped the golf cart momentarily at the gate. "So this is the Charlotte Street entrance. It wasn't always the main entrance. But Mrs. Somerton decided to make this the main entrance to the estate when she had the wall built. She also paid to have the street paved and lined with oaks for the community." Aubrey was easy to talk to, he thought. He didn't have that experience with most girls. He smiled at the thought, his confidence growing. He tried to spin the wheel of the golf cart with a show of finesse, but the wheel stuck on his stomach. The golf cart lurched around. He cast an embarrassed glance at Aubrey. Other than holding onto the golf cart's roof handle, she didn't seem to notice.

"Mrs. Somerton was extremely well traveled." Gerard was best in his tour guide mode, so he continued.

"Europe, China, Japan, Egypt. She loved nature and hired the young, but well-renowned, Frank Hadaway to design her gardens for her. She kind of had a project every year or two. Do you want to see the gardens in the order we get to them or the in the order they were built?"

"It would probably be easier just to see them in the order we get to them," Aubrey said, trying not to be a bother.

"Okay then, we see the Rock Garden first even though it was built last."

Gerard turned the golf cart to the left and down a narrow path toward a stand of trees. The number of trees and their placement was idyllic. If they had been arranged by nature, it was artfully done. They were some sort of pine, Aubrey noticed. The ground was rich with their red needles. As if by magic, a clearing fit for elves and sprites appeared. The entrance to a stone canyon, ruffled with ferns and jeweled with wild orchids, manifested itself. Miniature waterfalls flowed over boulders and into ponds laced with lily pads. Aubrey inhaled in surprise and awe.

"Beautiful isn't it?" Gerard didn't wait for a response. "We're only going past it today. Remember, just a general overview. We'll have time to do some serious exploring in the next couple days."

Aubrey found herself excited at the prospect. As Gerard drove past, Aubrey saw that in the midst of the fairytale landscape there stood a garden house, crafted entirely of stone. Saw-toothed crenellations along the top, and an arched window opening, gave it the air of a miniature castle. And sitting on the inside ledge of the window was the girl wearing the white lace dress. Her pale blonde hair was mounded and surrounded by a braid that continued over her shoulder, giving the impression of a bird's crest. The skirt of her dress fell casually over the window ledge. With its tiers of lace, it gave the impression of a white feathered tail.

"Coming into view on your right will be the carriage house, and right after that we'll pass the Old-Fashioned Garden. You can glimpse the mansion to your right through the trees."

Aubrey craned her neck, anticipating the next vista. But, captivated by the girl in the garden house, she looked back over her shoulder for a last glance. The girl was gone.

five

THE OLD-FASHIONED Garden's riotous plantings didn't suit Aubrey, but Gerard promised that, once in the throes of summer, its colors were like an impressionist's painting.

"We're missing the Blue and White Garden, the Pansy Garden, and the Moonlight Garden," Gerard said. "They're back there." He pointed to a place behind some trees. "Better seen on foot. They're quite intimate." He chuckled. "That means small," he said, in case Aubrey didn't see the humor in his little joke.

She could see they were passing behind the mansion now, and by following along on the map with her finger, she could see how the next several gardens backed up to one another. She noticed how the flat side of the semi-circular Rose Garden was bordered by a vine-covered pergola that hemmed in the right side of the ornate Italian Garden, which had taken her breath away just an hour or so ago. They passed tall hedges, which Gerard told her surrounded the Hidden Garden with its elaborate fountains and benches.

They rounded another corner, and Gerard stopped the golf cart beside a doorway in a brick wall.

"This is worth seeing," he said.

Aubrey followed him through the doorway into a ruin. They were standing alongside a built-in swimming pool open to the sky. It was empty except for some rain water and sludge at the bottom of the deep end. The floor and walls of the pool were cracking, and nature was trying desperately to retake what was once hers. Surrounding the pool was a walkway whose roof was held up by Corinthian columns.

"This is a wreck!" Aubrey said. "What *is* this place?"

"These are the Roman baths," Gerard said, calmly. "Yeah, they are a wreck, but a magnificent wreck when you consider the pool was built in 1890, was heated, and the water was piped two miles from the lake to fill the pool every couple days."

Aubrey had to agree. Those facts did make it quite amazing.

They finished the overview with a drive past the Japanese Garden with its meandering streams, moon-bridge, red tea house, and a view of the vast lawns where deer once grazed.

"What is that?" Aubrey pointed to another small stone structure. It looked like another castle with squared turrets and crenellations at the top. But it was narrow, only a little deeper than a façade. Behind it, in the lawn,

Aubrey noticed what seemed to be a circular foundation.

Gerard stopped the golf cart and rested his wrist on the steering wheel. "That is what is left of the aviary. It's the peacock house. See those stones in the lawn?"

Aubrey nodded and waited for his explanation.

"That once was the foundation of the domed flying cage. It was huge. There were other buildings that housed the birds, but this was their yard."

"You mentioned peacocks?"

"Mmm-hmmm. Mrs. Somerton loved peacocks, but especially white ones. She had several."

"Was that one of them back in the parlor – stuffed?" Aubrey asked, thinking of the one she nearly touched.

"Yes." Gerard started the golf cart and drove the short distance, ending in the same place they had started just facing the opposite direction, in front of the old carriage house. "Taxidermy was a hobby among the rich at the time," he said over the purr of the idling motor.

Oh, Aubrey thought, that explains the dead stuffed zoo back at the house.

"Let's go see what Ida has planned for you now." Gerard dislodged himself from behind the steering wheel. Silently, they walked the short distance to the house in the early afternoon sunshine. Aubrey realized there was a newfound spring in her step. The weather was getting warmer. School was ending soon. She just had to get through exams. She would work here all summer. She wouldn't get paid, but it was a necessary step toward college. For once, things were looking pretty good, and, despite her mother's attempts to make things otherwise, she was making them all happen by herself.

She looked up at the imposing home with its turrets and verandas. At the far end of the end of the mansion, on one of those verandas, she noticed the girl in the long white dress standing at the stone railing. Is this one of those places where volunteers dressed up in period costumes, she wondered? No one had mentioned it....

"Gerard?" The sight of the girl had halted Aubrey at the base of the eight stone steps leading to the mansion's main entrance. But Gerard had already begun his short jog up to the double wooden doors propped open to the sunshine. He turned in response to Aubrey's call just as she decided it was more important to catch up than to point out the girl. She jogged up the steps in his wake.

Later, when Gerard had to recount the incident, he wasn't sure if Aubrey had tripped or simply missed a step. He just saw Aubrey's feet falter before she fell backwards, and as he was in front of her, there was nothing he could do to stop her from tumbling backwards down the steps. He heard the crack of her head on the sidewalk.

"Ida! Ida! Help! Anybody!" he yelled as he raced down the steps to where Aubrey lay like a rag doll.

He heard someone shriek, "Oh, my!"

"Get help!" he yelled again over his shoulder, without looking to whom he was talking. "She fell!" His hands shook as he tried to remember what to do. Only "what *not* to do" ricocheted against his brain. *Don't move her. Don't move her.*

"Where are the paramedics? C'mon!" he yelled in

frustration. "Don't worry, Aubrey," he said more quietly to her. There was no response. "We're getting help. They're coming." He tried to speak reassuringly to her, then turned his head and yelled toward the door. "Ida? Are they coming? Did you call?"

"They said they're on their way," Ida replied in a shaky voice. She made her way daintily down the steps, using the stone railing for a guide. "Oh, my. Oh my…" She leaned over Aubrey and Gerard. "Oh, this isn't good."

"She hit her head," Gerard repeated, wanting to turn Aubrey, to lay her more comfortably, but knowing he shouldn't. "She hasn't opened her eyes, Ida. Aubrey, Aubrey, can you hear me? C'mon, Aubrey, open your eyes."

"How did it happen?" Ida asked bending over Aubrey, hearing sirens in the distance.

"Here they come," Gerard said to Aubrey. "I don't know, Ida. She must have lost her footing. She just all of a sudden fell backwards."

AUBREY WASN'T SURE how it happened either, but she knew something, or more accurately someone, had run into her. She hadn't seen anyone, but that was what that moment had felt like – like someone had shouldered her out of the way. She could barely hear, or open her eyes, or move, and her thoughts – her consciousness – was in an odd place. It was drifting somewhere half in dark and half in light. The world she knew seemed quiet and foggy, but there was a place that was nearer, clearer. In the part that was light, she saw the girl in white bend over her and study her with intensely pale blue eyes.

"Come with me," the girl said. She offered Aubrey a hand to help her up. Aubrey took it, sat up, and got to her feet. She dusted herself off. Aubrey looked to the place she had been lying. There was no sign of Gerard or Ida. No sound of sirens.

"Am I dead?" Aubrey asked.

"Don't be ridiculous." The girl gave a comforting smile. "But I am. I think I was murdered."

Six

"YOU'RE A ghost?" Aubrey asked as they walked along the house toward the Italian Garden, the day bathed in an intensely white sun light.

"I prefer the term 'shade'," the girl said. "I think my mother would as well. She liked Greek things." The girl glided with stately elegance down the wide walkway as if she had strolled there every day of her life. She turned left at the fountain and headed toward the back of the garden. Aubrey hadn't noticed that the walkway continued along the cedar trees. They followed the path behind a columned and iron-domed garden house to the Japanese Garden.

"Forgive me, my name is Maeve," the girl said, smiling kindly.

"I'm –"

"Au-*brey*. I know." She gave a shy smile.

Aubrey wanted to question Maeve, but something prevented her. All she could do was follow. Maeve led, just a few steps ahead, at a leisurely pace. They continued walking through a red tori arch, following a narrow winding path along the undulating terrain. Maeve guided them to the stone moon bridge. It was a small semi-circular bridge, whose reflection on the rivulet below completed a perfect circle, like a moon. At the bridge's apex, carved into the stone were two seats, one on each side of the bridge. Maeve perched herself on one side and gestured to Aubrey, who settled opposite. For the first time, Aubrey really looked at Maeve realizing she was oddly translucent. She studied her as an awkward silence filled the void between them.

Maeve had the posture of royalty, her hands folded in her lap, her eyes downcast. Her skin was pale, her cheekbones high, her mouth just a little too wide for her face. Her ivory hair glowed with the brilliance of a winter sun. She was stunningly beautiful, and yet, Aubrey was sure she saw pain in her countenance.

Aubrey's mind floated with a barrage of questions, and managed to focus on one. "So, I'm not dead?"

Maeve's eyes met hers and widened with sympathy. "Oh, no, definitely not."

"Then where am I? What happened?" Aubrey was confused, but it wasn't overwhelming. In the lightness and darkness of her mind, there was a peacefulness.

"Well, I invited you here, and you followed." Maeve paused. "But you're still there, too."

"But…Maeve," Aubrey used the name hesitantly. "I wasn't on the sidewalk when I looked back. I fell. Where am I?"

"You're there. I'm sure they're taking care of you.

You're not dead, or you'd be somewhere else. Not here," she said vaguely.

Aubrey glanced around the Japanese Garden that she and Gerard had driven past only a half hour ago. It was the same, but different. The white and red tea house looked like it was ready to welcome guests on a hot summer day, not – preserved – as it had looked when they passed it. The plantings looked fresher and younger, the pond banks tended.

"Not dead," Aubrey said. It wasn't a question. More a coming-to-grips.

"No," Maeve confirmed.

"But you are."

"Yes."

"And that makes me?"

"A shadow?" Maeve suggested.

"Can people see me? There *are* people here?"

"Oh, yes. There are people here. My family, the workers. This is where I live." Maeve beamed as she looked around her. Suddenly, she looked distant. "Lived," she corrected. She cleared her throat and her eyes flashed an apology. "I don't know if they can see you. I've never tried this before." She raised a surprised eyebrow. "I wasn't positive it would work."

"I guess it did," Aubrey touched the stone of the bridge next to her. It was rough and cold under her fingers. It was real.

"You seem calm about this," Maeve said. "I'm glad. I didn't want to upset you."

"I feel like calm is all I *can* be," Aubrey said. "I feel

like my energy is somewhere else."

THE NURSE PULLED ON fresh gloves as she entered the ICU cubical. Aubrey lay unmoving on the bed, the ventilator pumping rhythmically, heart monitors beeping. Her mother, Lenora, leaned against the institutional-peach wall, gathering her apprehension and her sweater around her. She *knew* Aubrey shouldn't have taken the position at Fairview. Don't ask her how she knew, she just knew. In cases like this, for other people's sake, she called it her "mother's intuition," but she knew it went much deeper than that.

That morning, they had had a fight about Aubrey's decision. Not really a fight. Words.

"I really wish you would consider another option," she had said sternly while pouring Aubrey's cereal. "All the kids like volunteering at the SPCA."

Aubrey's retort had been logical. "You *know* I'm allergic to animals. Why can't you just let me try it my way?"

"I just have a feeling about this," her mother had said through clenched teeth. She had closed her eyes to the possibilities she saw.

"What? Your super senses?" Aubrey had spit the words. "Don't pull the medium crap with me, mom. You're a fake and we both know it." Aubrey had picked up her book bag and stormed out of the house, her cereal uneaten.

Well, they had tried it her way and look what happened. Maybe most days she did exaggerate her abilities but *this* – Lenora had known it would be disastrous. She needed a hug. She needed to hug Aubrey. But neither one of those things would happen right now. All she could do was watch the machine breathe for her daughter and hope that all of Aubrey's energy was going toward healing herself.

Seven

"SO WHY DID you...invite me here?" Aubrey asked.

Maeve smoothed the skirt of her dress over her lap and then played with an edge of lace before answering. "I suppose it was simply because I needed assistance."

"Assistance?"

"Yes. Since I..." She looked uncomfortable. "Since I...*died*, there are things I can do, but there are many things I cannot do, cannot see. I never imagined there would be barriers, but there are. I need someone to help figure out what happened to me. I don't think I was supposed to die so soon."

"And for some reason you think I will be able to help figure that out?"

"You felt me in the house. You saw me. No one else has done that, not really," Maeve said. "That woman says the house is haunted, but no one has really seen me – until now."

"Lucky me."

"No! Lucky me!"

"But how can *I* help?"

"I am not quite sure. We need to know first if you can be seen. Then we will decide how you can help. Let's go back to the house and put you in some reasonable clothing in case someone does see you. They certainly can't see you like *that*!" Maeve eyed Aubrey's black jeans, red polo, and flowered canvas sneakers. She chuckled. "You certainly dress oddly. More like a boy than a girl."

"We've come a long way," Aubrey said under her breath. But Maeve was already making her way back toward the tori arch. There was a determination in her movements now.

"Come along," Maeve called, and when Aubrey had caught up she continued. "You can wear one of my older dresses. Mother has wanted me to wear white for the last year or so. It's all the fashion. I'm sure she doesn't remember my older dresses. And they're really quite wonderful still. If people can see you, we'll pack a bag for you, and we'll pretend you are one of my chums from school come to visit. You haven't heard about my – what happened to me. Your ride will have already departed, and you'll be stranded here. Mother won't turn her back on you. You can stay for a few days and help me puzzle this all out."

"You have this all planned, don't you," Aubrey

observed.

Maeve ignored the comment. "We'll have to fix that hair. Why did you do that to it? I suppose if we put it in a bun we can hide that horrid red."

Aubrey decided to ignore that comment. She wasn't sure she liked this girl. But what choice did she have? She tagged along, struggling all the while to organize thoughts that whirled in front of her and then flitted away quicker than hummingbirds. What had happened to her? Oh yeah. She fell. She must be in a hospital? So was this a dream? Maybe. Maybe she didn't have to take any of this seriously. But things felt real. Like this walk. It was long. She was getting tired, winded.

Maeve led her across the estate's main drive to the house. They passed a man unloading flowering plants from a wheelbarrow.

"Good morning, Gus," Maeve said to him as they passed. The man acted like he didn't hear or see her. Aubrey passed unnoticed as well.

"I think that's a good sign for now." Maeve said and allowed Aubrey to fall into step alongside her. "At least no one can see that outfit of yours. Let's make you more presentable." Maeve led the way into and through the house to the main staircase. Aubrey noticed furniture arrangements were different, and upholstery was fresh and plush.

Upstairs in Maeve's room, Aubrey sat, as directed, on a tufted settee. "You'll need the proper undergarments, and here are a few dresses to choose from." Her voice was muffled from inside the closet. She emerged bearing armloads of fabric, which she proudly dumped on the bed. She helped Aubrey into the undergarments, laughing at her unfamiliarity with chemises, corsets, combinations and petticoats.

"For Pete's sake!" Aubrey exhaled. "All this and I'm not dressed *yet*?"

"Of course not!" Maeve chided. "Haven't you heard of modesty? Now, I think this dress might be your best choice for a travelling dress." She struggled Aubrey's head and arms through the chosen outfit.

"This is so heavy. No wonder all you girls did was sit around and sew," Aubrey mused. Maeve was right behind her. She could feel the gentle tug as Maeve did up the buttons on the dress's back. She should have been able to feel Maeve's breath, she was so close, and when Maeve spoke her voice was soft. Maeve was practically whispering in Aubrey's ear.

"Oh, that's not what life was like at all. Of course, I spent many hours with my needlework. And I love to read," she added. "That's expected. But there was so much more to life here at Fairview. My cousins would come to visit, or Mother and Father would host parties, and their guests would bring their children. There is a pool, you know, and a bowling alley. We have a stage on the third floor in the children's wing! Sometimes there would be several croquet games occurring at the same time, and with all the gardens, why, we'd drive Mother to her wit's end with our turns at hide and seek – "

Maeve's fingers finished with the last button, and Aubrey turned slowly to face her. "It sounds like this place could be a lot of fun," Aubrey said quietly.

"Oh, it is –" Maeve caught herself. "It *was* wondrous fun," she said wistfully.

"THIS ISN'T MUCH FUN," Pitch said as Lenora held the yellow papery gown. Pitch pulled his arms through the lemonade-colored hospital garb as Lenora tugged it over his shoulders and began tying it behind his back. Intermittent beeping and suctioning sounds attacked him from all sides. He glanced nervously around – everywhere but through the glass in front of him.

Aubrey was in there. *His* Aubrey. And she didn't realize what she meant to him. Even he hadn't realized it, until recently. It had happened all of a sudden. He couldn't pinpoint the moment when things had changed for him – when her friendship wasn't enough. And instead of talking to her about it, he drove away in frustration that morning. All because he was afraid of losing her. And now, *this*.

Nurses busied themselves at computer screens behind a hub that served as the nerve center in the middle of the room. One nurse, wearing a surgical suit on which images of Winnie-the-Pooh characters tumbled, walked toward them. Quickly but calmly she began to punch information into a computer monitor at a station outside the glass doorway. Pitch looked down at his paper gown. It felt awkward – too crisp, too unreal. Like this place.

He had never been in a hospital before, let alone an Intensive Care Unit.

Lenora patted him gently on the shoulder. He had forgotten she was there.

He turned to her with a sheepish grin. "If the kids at school could see me now." How long could he put this off?

She seemed to sense his apprehension.

"It's okay, Oliver," Lenora said. "I just go in and talk to her. Just as if she were awake."

"But what do you talk about?"

"Anything. Everything. I imagine she's answering me."

Pitch nodded and, with his eyes downcast, entered Aubrey's glass room. He always had things to talk about with Aubrey. The day bounced around in his head. How he spilled blue paint on his best ripped black jeans. How bad the tacos looked at lunch today. How Mrs. Wilson's Pekinese, Mitzie, threw up on his sneakers during their walk after school. How he tripped going up the stairs on the way to science lab.

He took a deep breath and looked at his best friend, who meant more to him than she knew. Aubrey looked so small in the bed with all the tubes and wires coming out of her. The white blanket was pulled up to her chest, but her arms were laying limply at her sides on top of the covers.

"Hello Aubrey," he said and gently slipped his fingers under her hand. Wrapping his fingers around her hand, he gave it a gentle squeeze.

"Mitzie threw up on my sneakers this afternoon while I was walking her." He waited for a reaction that didn't come. "It was horrendous at the time. But after I cleaned it up, I couldn't stop laughing – you know – that laugh when you just can't stop? If you were there you would have died –"

Pitch stopped short. *Oh God! How could I have said that to her?* He promised himself, right there on the spot, that if she came back to them, he'd let her make up her own mind about their – friendship.

Eight

AUBREY STOOD outside Fairview's main double doors. Slowly it came to her that she was standing on the landing at the top of the stairs where she fell. Cautiously, she glanced at the bottom of the stairs, half expecting to see herself lying there. Nothing. So, instead, she gripped the heavy suitcase in both hands. She bounced it lightly against her knees as she waited. One hand occasionally moved to her head to make sure her hat was staying put. She felt like Mary Poppins. To the west, the sky behind the trees darkened into evil-looking cotton candy clouds that rumbled with thunder.

Nearby, Maeve clasped her hands, and began a delicate childlike spring on her toes. "Oh, a thunderstorm!" she said gleefully. "How I love thunderstorms." Aubrey, noticing she didn't have an umbrella, looked sourly at Maeve's translucent figure and turned the doorbell key.

The door opened as the first drops of rain began to fall. In the flash of lightning, Aubrey could see they were large, fat drops that left healthy spots on the stone at her feet.

"Why, hello Miss." A servant girl greeted her.

"Hello," Aubrey began hesitantly.

Maeve nodded her encouragement. "They can see you now. I wonder if it's the clothes."

Knowing she couldn't continue a conversation with Maeve, she focused her attention on the servant.

"I'm Aubrey Harrison." She waited for the recognition that she knew would not come. Maeve had told her this would be important to making the plan seem authentic. True to Maeve's guess, the girl looked confused. The drops of rain were increasing in number around Aubrey.

"Maeve's chum from Brayden," Aubrey recited. Again she waited while the servant's face showed increasing dread. "She invited me to stay for a few weeks this summer."

"Oh, my," the young girl gasped. The sky opened and a torrent of rain issued forth. "Come in, come in." Her voice was panicked with confusion. "But stay here, please. I need to get Mrs. Somerton."

Aubrey stood just inside the door for what seemed like an eternity with Maeve at her side whispering encouragements.

"Don't worry. She's explaining things to Mother. Let me see what's happening." She drifted off leaving Aubrey dripping near the door.

Down the hall, Claire Somerton was sitting on the sofa in her study while the servant handed her a glass of water.

"...says her name is Aubrey Harrison, and she's a friend of Maeve's from school. Ma'am, it doesn't sound like she knows. She says Maeve invited her to stay a few weeks, and she's got her luggage with her."

Maeve saw her mother sip the water and gingerly place the glass on a table in front of the sofa. Her mother stared at the glass while she spoke.

"Has her ride departed?"

"I believe so, Ma'am."

"Then I shall speak with her. Tell her to wait in the salon, and I will be there momentarily."

"Yes ma'am," the servant girl said, and she left Claire Somerton alone. Maeve watched as her mother covered her face with her hands. Her shoulders shook slightly. After a while, she dropped her hands to her lap and sighed, dried her hands on her skirt with the pretense of straightening it, got up and walked to the window. She stared out onto the grounds, steeling herself, and Maeve watched, forlorn, as her Mother turned to make her way to the salon.

Aubrey seated herself on the sofa in the salon as the servant had directed. She recognized this room as the one where she had first met Ida, the one with the round alcove where the white stuffed peacock was perched on the porcelain garden table. She had noticed when she entered the room that the peacock was not there, nor was the garden table. Instead, in the round alcove, there was a chair, a footstool, a small wooden table, and a lamp.

Claire Somerton entered the room.

"Stand up," Maeve suddenly hissed over Aubrey's shoulder.

Shocked by Maeve's sudden appearance, Aubrey stood abruptly and clumsily offered her hand, trying to be respectful.

"Good day, Mrs. Somerton. I'm Aubrey Harrison," she said, as rehearsed.

"It's good to meet you Aubrey. It's always good to meet one of Maeve's friends."

"My apologies," Aubrey said trying her best not to sound like a product of the twenty-first century. "There seems to be some confusion..."

"Confusion...not exactly." Claire rolled a pearl of her necklace between her fingers. "I'm sorry. This has been a difficult time for us here at Fairview. You see, my daughter passed away a week ago." The woman, whose posture had been perfect up to this point, crumpled onto the sofa.

"No!" Aubrey gasped. She ran to Mrs. Somerton and sat beside her, automatically touching her arm in sympathy.

"My apologies," the woman said, straightening herself, not without effort.

"No, no, I'm the one who should be apologizing," Aubrey said. "How rude of me to come at such a...a..."

"Now, now," the woman said, misunderstanding Aubrey's faltering as shock and sorrow. "I am forgetting the news would be upsetting to you as well. Maeve's friends are always welcome here. I would appreciate your visit. There's no reason we couldn't get acquainted, and you could familiarize yourself with Maeve's home – she loved it here...." She began to dissolve again.

"I can see why she would," Aubrey said quietly, looking around at the almost familiar.

Claire paused, watching Aubrey wistfully. "How rude of me. Look, you're wet from the rain. Let's get you settled in your room. Lindsay!"

Claire rose. The servant girl appeared and attended to Aubrey's suitcase. She followed a short distance behind as Claire led Aubrey down the hall to the wide main staircase. "You'll have supper with me at seven," Claire directed over her shoulder. "I take breakfast at six. If that is too early for you, the staff can have breakfast ready later than that – you think about it, and we'll talk about the schedule at supper. I'm afraid you'll have to take dinner by yourself. I usually take it in my office while I am working."

At the top of the stairs, Claire stepped across the hall and placed the palm of her hand on the closed door of a room. Maeve's room, Aubrey remembered. Seeming to think better of it, she resumed walking down the hall. Aubrey noticed they had arrived in the section of the corridor that formed the arched gallery that looked over into the Great Hall. The three-story bank of windows was opposite them. Claire led Aubrey around the final edge of the gallery to the last door. It led to a small but tidy bedroom.

"I hope you'll be comfortable here. There is a bath

right behind." She pointed to a door Aubrey had assumed was a closet. "We welcome you to Fairview. Please treat it as your home." With that, Claire turned and left, Lindsay in tow.

"Well, that was awkward," Aubrey mumbled, hoisting her suitcase onto the bed. Claire Somerton had been polite enough, but her tone.... Aubrey tried to place the emotion behind it. It had sounded almost business-like. Not the tone of a woman whose only daughter had just died. Perhaps Claire Somerton was just a private person, she thought.

Aubrey looked around at the room. She noticed a dresser and a second door that must be the closet. She walked the few steps it took to return to the room's door, the hall's arched balcony stretched before her. Across the chasm of the Great Hall, in a doorway next to the massive fireplace chimney, in the entrance to the room where she put on the dress she now wore, stood a smiling, transparent Maeve. As one hand absently stroked the bear skin that hung over the railing in front of her, the other fanned a dainty wave to Aubrey before she faded.

Nine

AT FIVE MINUTES to seven, Aubrey descended the main staircase in a dress Maeve had chosen. She took the steps carefully, the length of her pink summer gown and the ruffles at its hem working against her. There was a small train, which Maeve had assured her was still on the cusp of fashion. For a moment, at the bottom of the staircase, Aubrey forgot her way. She nervously smoothed the lace sleeves of her dress, then remembered the dining room was to the left. When she entered the room, she couldn't believe her eyes. The table was laden with the finest china, silver, crystal, fresh flowers and candles. The layers of finery was a feast in itself. Aubrey hesitated in the archway.

"Sit here near me, Aubrey." Claire, who was seated at the head of the table, gestured to a seat to her right. Claire was dressed in black, but the beaded lace gown barely seemed mourning attire. Her blonde hair was scooped into an elaborate French twist that made her neck appear long and elegant. Aubrey noticed she again wore pearls.

A dapper man, who was sitting at the table with his back to Aubrey, turned as Claire spoke to her. His black hair, greying at the temples, was slicked into place. A neatly trimmed mustache danced above a pleasantly childish grin, and his dark eyes sparkled.

"Oh my, you must be the young lady who is Maeve's friend." He pushed his chair out to stand and take her hand. "Dalton Kendall." He made a slight bow. "Here, dear." He led her behind Claire's chair to the other side of the table and pulled the chair out for her. "My deepest sympathies to you. This all must be a shock to you. Claire tells me you only just found out about poor Maeve."

"Yes, thank you Mr. Kendall." Aubrey cast her eyes downward, hiding the grief that wasn't there.

"Please call me Dalton. All of my friends do."

"Dalton, you are such a solace to me," Claire said, lifting her wine glass to her lips. Dalton placed a reassuring hand on Claire's shoulder as he moved back to his seat. "Ah, and here is Frank." Another man had appeared in the doorway. Aubrey noticed he looked earthier than Dalton, as if he spent more time in the sun and wind. It was difficult to ascertain his age. He appeared to be significantly younger than Dalton, maybe late twenties, yet the deep wrinkles at the corners of his eyes made him seem much older. He ran a hand through his brown hair to suggest that it behave. His tweed jacket and brown pants, although neat and clean, seemed a cut below Dalton's tailored black suit.

"Dalton, Claire. I hope I haven't kept you." With just a few steps, the man Dalton called Frank strode to Claire at the head of the table, took her hand and brought it to his lips. Aubrey was at the perfect angle to see the deep dimple from his roguish grin and the glint of his green eyes from under his long lashes as he glimpsed Claire's cautious gaze. As the seats to the right and left of Claire were taken, Frank took the seat next to Aubrey.

"And who is your newest guest, Claire?" he asked, turning his smile in Aubrey's direction. Aubrey realized it wasn't just his clothes that seemed out of place. His countenance did as well. This was a house that was supposed to be in mourning, and he was acting as if he had missed that point.

"Frank, this is Aubrey Harrison. She was Maeve's friend from school. She just arrived this afternoon. She's just heard the news."

"Ah." He pulled a serious mask over his face. "How truly sorry I am to hear of your loss." He didn't look or sound truly sorry, Aubrey thought.

"Thank you, sir," Aubrey said, hoping to sound like she belonged.

Frank chuckled. "You don't need to *sir* anyone at Fairview. Isn't that right, Claire? We're all equals. Family." His playfulness returned.

Claire put her wine glass down with what Aubrey suspected was aggravation. "The girl was just trying to be polite Frank. They're taught that at Brayden."

"Ah, my apologies again, dear."

His tone was polite enough, but Aubrey detected a tension developing in the room.

"Claire dear, you look lovely this evening. Mourning becomes you."

"Frank, that's enough." Dalton cut him off.

"I can take my meals in my room, Frank, but I prefer to have friends around me, some distraction, if that is all right with you." Aubrey noted sarcasm at the last comment.

"And which am I, dear? A friend or a distraction?"

Aubrey felt as if she were watching a tennis match, and she was glad when the first course was served, and the conversation turned to murmurs of gratitude. A servant, bearing a large tureen to the sideboard, ladled soup into small bowls and placed them in front of each diner. Aubrey noticed that Maeve had slipped into the chair next to Dalton.

"When did you get here?" Aubrey asked her.

"Get here?" Frank asked, mistaking the direction of her question. "I live on the estate, dear. I am the landscape architect hired to design the gardens that Claire so desperately desires surround Fairview. There's a nice little Tudor cottage on the grounds that I call home for now, isn't that right Claire?"

Maeve reached out a hand to the centerpiece and wistfully fingered a grape as if to pull it from the stem. She lifted her eyes to look across the table at Aubrey.

"I don't know what to think about him at this point," Maeve said. "He didn't seem so…I don't know…blatant before. He built me a garden house that looked like a castle. Mother loved it."

"I try to give the staff their individual space so they can maintain their own lives," Claire was explaining. Aubrey noticed the use of the word "staff" to describe Mr. Hadaway.

A servant removed the bowls and brought the next course – fresh vegetables on a plate. The meal continued through braised beef, delicate stuffed mushrooms, coffee, and petit fours. Somehow the conversation remained on the edge of civility. Aubrey listened and tried to field questions thrown her way without giving away the true state of affairs.

"Don't worry," Maeve interjected at one point when the conversation was getting bogged down over what Claire declared was a much-inflated price of a Katsura tree. "The men are going to retire to the porch soon for their cigars, and Mother will either go to her room or her office."

Maeve knew the routine well.

"Another wonderful meal, Claire," Dalton said, dabbing the corners of his mouth with his napkin before laying it next to his plate. "A cigar, Frank?"

Frank pushed his chair away from the table in agreement. "Yes. A good evening to you, Claire."

She did not respond, but instead traced the etching on the foot of her wine glass. After the men left Claire said, "Aubrey, I am afraid I am not the best of company these days. I will do my best to amuse you while you are here, but we will need to get in touch with your family and let them know…well, know that there is really no reason for your visit – considering the circumstances." She glanced up, and Aubrey was sure she saw an apology in her dark eyes.

"I usually retire after supper," Claire continued, and she, too, now rose to leave the table. "Maeve knew how to entertain herself. Will you be all right? Sometimes a stroll through one of the gardens can be relaxing this time of night. That's what they are there for, but don't wander too far, unattended."

"Thank you, ma'am," Aubrey said. "Perhaps I will."

"We'll have breakfast tomorrow in The Bower." She gestured behind herself to a wall of glass doors that led to an outdoor area hung with vines.

Aubrey smiled her understanding. "Good night, then?"

"Yes, good night, child."

Aubrey found her way through Fairview to the library, whose screen door led to the veranda that wrapped the home like a shawl. The summer evening's warm air called to her. She considered sitting in one of the many wicker chairs, but she was too restless. Aubrey padded softly down the stairs in Maeve's old leather shoes to Claire's Blue and White garden, which led to the more secluded Night Garden. There, servants had lit candles among the aromatic white night-blooming cereus that glowed in the twilight. She settled herself on a stone bench set in a marble alcove at the back of the small floral room. Water splashed and bubbled in a small fountain where stone cherubs played. From here she could look back on Fairview. In the distance, she could see the silhouettes of Dalton and Frank and the glow of their cigars as they undoubtedly sipped expensive brandy and discussed the business of continued improvements to the estate. But she could also see Claire, who, above them, leaned against the railing of the veranda outside her bedroom, gazing at the perfected version of nature she forced men to create.

Ten

BREAKFAST THE next morning was not the gastro disaster Aubrey was expecting. Another meal like last night's and she would surely explode, she thought. Aubrey entered the dining room astonished to see a very vacant table. It was then she noticed the open glass doors to her right, slid accordion-style so that the wall of the dining room all but disappeared. The vast opening led to "The Bower" as Claire called it, an open space walled off by a high wrought iron frame and overhung with flowering vines. A marble lion's head spewed water into a small pool. As Aubrey sat at the table in another dress chosen by Maeve, breakfast was simply brought to her on a plate. A poached egg on toast and a bowl of soft, warm fruit – plums, she decided. It was light and delicious.

Claire sat like a fixture at her place at the end of the

table. Other than a polite but sterile "good morning" when Aubrey joined her, the only other sounds from Claire were sips from a hand-painted china cup and crumplings as she folded and refolded the newspaper she was reading. It was the headlines that were screaming, Aubrey noticed:

Triangle Shirtwaist Fire Aftermath
New Safety Laws Eyed
Investigating Commission Created

"Hmph," Claire finally said, laying down the paper with gentile force. "I know the fire was a catastrophe, but do we really need the government sticking their nose in?" she said to no one in particular. "Good morning, Dalton," she added as he entered The Bower.

Looking as smart as he did the previous night, Dalton had returned for breakfast. "Good morning, Claire, Aubrey." He seated himself and, as if on cue, a servant appeared with a plate similar to Aubrey's.

"These new safety regulations, Dalton, I know they're aimed at the factories, but how long until they are more widespread?" Claire said tapping the headlines with a finger. "Regulations are always so...complicated."

"That's dreadful breakfast talk, Claire," he criticized as he took a bite of egg. "Those factory folks have a lot to learn. Long hours, dangerous conditions. People getting killed – see Claire, not appropriate table talk. I'm losing my appetite, and this breakfast was looking delightful." The servant appeared again placing a plate of biscuits on the table.

Claire turned her attention to Aubrey ignoring Dalton's fallen face. "The help are happy here. Early this morning – every morning for that matter, workers line up at Fairview's gate – day workers. We have salaried people, but these are workers from the town, people anxious to work here. They know we pay well, treat them well." She didn't need to prove anything to Aubrey, and yet her tone implied that she did. It was tinged with frustration – or was it rationalization?

"Everything you are eating here, Aubrey, was made or grown right here on the estate – the eggs, the butter, the plums were even grown in the greenhouses. And all the employees get to take advantage of that as well. There is an employee hall where they take their meals. If they leave the property, well, then they're on their own, but as long as they are here on the grounds I take care of them. Don't I, Dalton?" A servant removed Claire's empty plate.

"Of course you do, dear," he responded while chewing, his appetite apparently revived. Dalton didn't look up from his food. Even if he had, he wouldn't have noticed Maeve glide into The Bower and sit on the edge of the fountain pool.

Aubrey was starting to notice it was all business all the time at Fairview. Maeve, who was flicking her unsubstantial fingers in the water trying to make it ripple, would have been used to this kind of conversation, but Aubrey wasn't. Maeve looked at Aubrey with sad eyes.

It was at that moment that it dawned on Aubrey that

maybe she shouldn't be tuning out. Maybe there would be hints or clues to help Maeve. And if she ever wanted to get back home – if she *could* ever get back home – she apparently had to do what she was brought here to do. Aubrey decided she needed to get down to business, too. Maeve smiled at her as if reading her mind.

"I would love to see where the food is grown," Aubrey said, in an attempt to steer the conversation to an end that might yield fruit of its own.

"Oh! That could be arranged. Dalton?" Claire smiled up at him. Aubrey noticed that just talking about the wonders of the estate changed Claire's tone and demeanor. She was proud of the place and enjoyed showing it off. Aubrey made a mental note of that.

"Of course, dear," Dalton responded. "How about right after breakfast, Aubrey? I always find that a morning stroll is good for the constitution."

"That sounds wonderful, Mr. Kendall."

"Dalton, please," he corrected with a warm smile.

"That sounds wonderful, Dalton." Aubrey grinned sheepishly behind her lashes. She ate another bite of stewed plums. She noticed a servant enter The Bower but stand along the wall holding a silver tea pot.

"And Aubrey, you are always welcome to explore the grounds on your own. Maeve would disappear for hours at a time. She loved to sketch, as you probably know." Claire wiped at something just below her eye.

"Yes, her drawings were wonderful," Aubrey improvised.

"Well, I don't know about that, but she certainly

practiced enough." Claire had a way of pulling herself together quickly, Aubrey noticed. Was that just her way, or did she feel that was the way she should behave as The Lady of Fairview?

"She kept a sketch book and pencils on the writing table in the library. You are welcome to add to it. She even had some colored pencils, I believe, and some water color paints. How are your skills?"

"I actually love my art classes," Aubrey said. "One of my paintings was in a show."

The confused look on Claire's face, warned Aubrey she had said too much.

"A show? At your age? How…wonderful. Where?"

"Uh, oh. Just at school," Aubrey stammered.

"I didn't realize Brayton displayed student work." Claire's voice trailed off as she sipped from her tea cup that had been subtly refilled by the servant during the conversation.

Eleven

"D ALTON?"

"Yes, Aubrey?" Their fine leather shoes made soft sounds on the well-worn path.

"Pardon me if I am being too bold, but...," she hesitated. "How are you connected here? To the Somertons and Fairview?"

They strolled along a narrow path flanked by a variety of trees. Dalton's steps were aided by a silver tipped walking stick, but the question of whether it was necessary or just for show would go unanswered for now. There were more pressing matters.

"Ah, yes." Dalton looked ahead down the winding path dappled with sunlight. A bird called out nearby. "It didn't occur to me that perhaps Maeve might not have mentioned me."

"Oh, I..."

"Don't apologize." He politely cut her off. She hadn't

intended to. "I am – was – Claire's husband's best friend. Edgar died almost two years ago. Claire was devastated. She had to mourn the loss of her husband, and her best friend," he added as an aside, "and also take his place running the estate. I stayed nearby as a friend, a consultant. I was always here anyway." He paused to give a seemingly apologetic smile. "Edgar and I always talked business about the estate. After his death, Claire wanted to run things. She had ideas of her own. She was just getting her feet under her. And now this – losing Maeve."

Aubrey looked away, through the trees to her right that bordered the fine manicured lawn. She wondered where Maeve had gone off to.

"I'm sorry if I upset you." Dalton's voice was kind, misinterpreting her silence.

"No…" Aubrey tried not to protest too much. She had her answer, and she was learning to play the part.

The distant clip clopping of hooves announced a wagonload of men on the estate's main road up ahead. She could see they wore grey work clothes. Some wore suspenders, all wore hats. They were chatting loudly and laughing, and as their paths converged, Aubrey noticed they spanned quite a range of ages, some possibly as young – or younger – than she, some as old as Dalton.

"'Lo, Mr. Kendall," one man said, doffing his cap in Dalton's direction.

"Men," Dalton greeted, bowing his head and touching the rim of his bowler.

The wagonload of men rolled past. Aubrey and

Dalton crossed the road to another path. Just ahead, the glitter of a thousand panes of glass forced her to look away.

"Hah!" Dalton caught her reaction. "Yes! It can be blinding at certain times of the day!"

Aubrey shaded her eyes with her arm. Through the glares and reflections, she saw a sprawling collection of glass buildings surrounding a giant, domed, glass house.

"Fairview's greenhouses!" Dalton announced with a flourish, and he picked up his pace. "Come! Come!"

Aubrey quickened her step to match his animated one. She marveled at how these people loved to show off what they had. But when Dalton opened the paned door to one wing of the complex, she squashed her judgement. What lay before her was truly an accomplishment. She wasn't sure what she noticed first – the moist heat of the room or the lush trees and plants. The environment was obviously what the vegetation craved. They all seemed to be reaching for the sunlight pouring through the ubiquitous panes.

"My, you can practically hear the plants growing!" Aubrey said.

"Yes! Yes!" Dalton practically danced to a tree dripping with fruit. "These are where your breakfast plums grew!"

"Oh, my! How wonderful! And what on Earth…?" Aubrey pointed to vines climbing the walls and roof of the greenhouse, hung heavy with crusty tan orbs.

"Muskmelons," Dalton informed.

"But they have little hammocks!" Aubrey said, very

amused.

"Ah, yes! The gardeners discovered that by making a little cheesecloth hammock for each melon, as it ripened, it did not risk falling and bruising."

"How very clever!" Aubrey agreed.

Dalton nodded and glanced around looking for the next treasure to share. Aubrey, too, looked around, carefully noticing all the shapes, textures, and shades of the crowded vegetation.

During their moment of quiet appreciation, off in the distance, Aubrey heard a shrill noise pierce the silence. The noise was long, then followed by four shorter bursts, just as shrill. It sounded like her gym teacher's whistle, she thought. She noticed concern register in Dalton's drawn brows. He had heard it, too.

"Oh, no...," he said, and Aubrey thought she heard him curse under his breath. Seemingly without a thought for her, he ran for the door, flung it open, and sprinted across the lawn, not caring to stay to the path. He held his walking stick like a runner's baton.

Aubrey quickly followed him out the door, and gathering up her skirts as best she could, ran after him. Maeve's leather shoes pinched, fighting her every step. She did her best to catch up. She could feel her hair spilling its pins, and she kept losing hold of her skirts. She was losing Dalton in the trees up ahead, but somehow, a memory of where she needed to go flashed on the movie screen of her mind. At some point, she had travelled this path before. He was running toward the Rock Garden.

She could hear the commotion before she could see it: men hollering loudly over each other. And as Aubrey crested the hill that overlooked the rocky glen, she saw several men running to and from the epicenter of the commotion. Over the men's yelling and running, wound through like a wild animal's cry, was the most horrid part moaning, part screaming Aubrey had ever heard. She drew her hands to her mouth to stifle her own cry when she saw the young boy whose tortured sounds were the center of the scene. He lay partially pinned beneath a boulder. Men brought boards. By crafting crude levers, they pried the boulder up and off of him. But the boy's wails only grew wilder.

Aubrey's view of the boy became blocked as the men surrounded him. She saw Dalton, who was flanked by several of the workers, carry the boy down the path to a wagon, which had appeared on the nearest road.

"What happened, I didn't see –" said one of the remaining men, visibly shaken.

"Just slipped on the muddy embankment," another man said quietly. "Could have happened to any of us."

Aubrey watched from the knoll as the knot of men waited.

Dalton returned only after the wagon careened from the scene. His pace was slower than when he left, and the men rushed to him. He talked quietly to them for a few minutes before they fled, heading for the outbuilding that served as the infirmary. He looked up and found Aubrey staring at him from across the glen. He walked a short distance toward her, but collapsed onto an outcropping of rock. The only sounds came from a tiny waterfall that splashed into a nearby pond edged with pink water lilies and ferns. Its beauty defied the remnants of the horrible nearby scene. Aubrey crossed the garden and paused near the infamous boulder to pick up Dalton's walking stick. He had dropped it while he tended to the boy. She noticed the muddy trenches left by the heels and hands of a body that had lost its balance. She approached Dalton, whose fine suit was stained with blood and mud. She handed him his walking stick.

"Thank you," Dalton said. He laid it across his knees.

"Will he be all right?" Aubrey asked.

"We won't know until the doctor sees him. I don't think so, though." Dalton hung his head.

"Do the men know what happened?" she asked.

"He was moving the boulder. They had told him not to, that it was too heavy for him. He tried anyway. Lost his footing."

"Oh." She didn't know what to say. Something she couldn't pinpoint seemed to be wrong.

"Did you know him?" Aubrey asked.

"No, no. He was just a worker."

Aubrey stared at the tiny ripples in the pond. One led to another, and then to another. She remembered the headlines of the newspaper Claire had been reading at breakfast. Wasn't this what the legislation was about? Were incidents like this another ripple in the pond? She tried to recall Ms. Widman's lessons, but they were clouded and dim. Surely she had paid attention, but they had seemed meaningless at the time.

Twelve

"ARE YOU *sure* it was an accident?" There was a tinge of panic in Claire's voice.

Aubrey had followed Dalton up to Fairview, rushing to keep up with him, so determined was his pace. She followed him all the way into the house, but hung back in the hallway when he entered Claire's study to relay the events as they had unfolded. Dalton seemed to have forgotten about her.

"Accident?" There was an ever so slight hesitation in his voice. Still, he maintained a tone of forced calm. "Of *course* it was an accident, Claire. What else could it have *been*?"

Yes, what else could it have been? What was Claire so worried about? It *had* been an accident. She had seen it with her own eyes.

Well, no, she hadn't actually. She had seen the aftermath. But the men who had been there had all maintained it as such. *Surely*, it hadn't been done on purpose. That would mean –

She ducked across the hall into the library, eager to lay her eyes on anything that would expunge the image of the young boy from her mind. She noticed a leather covered book and cloth bound package on the desk. She flipped open the book revealing colored pencil drawings and took it to be Maeve's sketchbook. As her fingers met the cloth package, they sensed the slender shape of pencils. Instead of leaving through the hallway, which still resonated with snippets of Claire's and Dalton's frantic discussion, she dashed out the library's door onto one of the home's many verandas.

Aubrey fled down the steps, running through the intimate Blue and White Garden just off the porch. The garden ended with a piece of stone architecture that was a combination wall and patio. Cherubs played in a low fountain, and a few feet away, a statue of the Roman goddess Diana was flanked by two stone benches. But these ornamentations faced the house, and Aubrey wanted no part of that place right now.

She skirted the patio heading into the next garden and found that the wall was two-sided. The back side also had two benches, although these were generous individual stone seats. Sitting on the furthest one, hunched over with his forearms resting on his knees, was a young man. He was staring at the ground.

"Oh!" She gasped, as much from being out of breath as from surprise.

He looked up. His shaggy blond hair was curled up

around his cap. He wore a white shirt with the cuffs rolled onto his forearms. The shirt was dirty from a morning's work. His brown pants were secured with suspenders.

"I'll leave you," Aubrey said, noticing the stranger looked distraught.

"I'm not supposed to be here," the young man said. He gathered himself and stood to leave.

Aubrey took in his work clothes and tried to piece together the situation. "You knew him," she finally realized out loud.

"Ben. Yes. He's dead."

"Dead? No – Please, sit," she finally directed, and he did, collapsing onto the stone seat and resuming his position of staring at the ground.

Aubrey dropped the book and pencils onto the closer stone seat and approached the young man. She squatted in front of him, her skirts billowing out around her. Even from this vantage point, he had to raise his head to look at her. He was sixteen or seventeen, she thought, and vaguely familiar.

"I'm Aubrey," she said quietly. "I'm sorry." The dirt on his face was streaked with tears. He buried his face in the crook of his arm and wiped his eyes.

"This is awkward," Aubrey said, standing. "You're obviously upset. I'll leave you."

"No, it's all right." He glanced around and added, as if it were an afterthought, "Isn't there someone with you?"

"With me?" Aubrey glanced around, and realized

that Maeve was drifting among the blooms in the nearby Blue and White Garden, casting glances their way as she dipped her head to sniff the flowers' fragrances. He couldn't see her, could he?

"The ladies visiting Fairview are usually chaperoned," he said, explaining himself.

She laughed lightly. "Oh, no. They've given me the run of the place. I am – was – a friend of Maeve's…"

"Oh, God." He buried his face in his hands. "And now it's happened again. It keeps happening. I feel like there's something wrong here."

"Wrong *here*?"

He took her confusion as criticism. His head shot up and his eyes, still wet, looked panicked. "I didn't mean that!"

Aubrey was spinning with the conversation. She seemed to be having a difficult time keeping the young man on one subject. She felt, as she had so many times in the last couple of days, to be losing control.

"Look," she said. "I couldn't say you said anything because I don't know who you are. I don't understand what you think is wrong, or what you are so panicked about. So I think it best that I just leave."

She bent to gather the sketchbook and pencils and turned in the direction she thought would take her to the Japanese Garden.

"He was a friend of mine, and I'd like to think Maeve was as well."

Aubrey turned and met his eyes. "You knew Maeve?" She glanced over his shoulder where Maeve still lingered.

He nodded.

There was a pause in the conversation before he continued. He inclined his head toward her art supplies.

"You were looking for a place to draw?"

"Yes."

"Let's walk. I'll show you a beautiful place." The way he was comfortable guiding her gave Aubrey a twinge of familiarity, but it was only a slight, unanchorable twinge.

HOW COULD HE HAVE let it happen to her? Gerard sat on the top step outside the front door of Fairview. He rested his head in his hands, elbows on his knees. Aubrey's fall played over and over in his mind. He couldn't have caught her, could he have? Could he have reacted faster? Maybe grabbed for her arm or wrist?

He ran his hand through his short thick blond curls. A smile played at the corners of his lips for just a second as he remembered seeing her for the first time – how Aubrey had fallen at his feet when she entered Fairview. She had absolutely disarmed him. He didn't have much experience with girls, but he had been at his best with her, able to tell her all about the estate. The pleasant thought lasted only a moment, though. She hadn't noticed him. Not in the same way. And actually, thank goodness – his thoughts jumped – because there had been that embarrassing moment when he had gotten stuck behind the wheel of the golf cart.

His thoughts ricocheted. He had never felt so distraught, so guilty. He was full of self-loathing. He was awkward – socially inept. He was grossly out of shape. Maybe if he didn't look like this, if he was stronger. He was not at all the hero that Aubrey had needed that day. And now she was in a coma. He remembered jogging up the stairs ahead of her. Jogging. Who had he been kidding? He had been pathetically out of breath by the time he realized she had fallen. His only good trait – that he was intelligent – came off as being a self-absorbed know-it-all. He should have been concentrating on her. Had he been so intent on impressing her that he let it happen?

He doubted that she would ever talk to him again.

Thirteen

"YOU'RE not supposed to be talking to me, you know."

Aubrey glanced at the young man out of the corner of her eye as they walked.

He was only a little older than she was. Everyone else she had met on the estate had been a lot older, and conversations with them had been polite, but stilted. They had not yielded much information to help Maeve – or herself. Perhaps this young man would be able to fill in some of the details she was lacking.

"Here you are, alone with a boy, and you don't even know his name." His face, which had been so hung with grief, brightened slightly, but not without effort. His tone was teasing, but it was enough to make Aubrey remember where and when she was. He was talking about propriety.

"Oh, yes," she said. "I've introduced myself to you,

but you haven't introduced yourself to me."

"Well, Audrey, wasn't it? The name is Warren, if you think that solves the problem," he said, the light slipping from his face once again. He doffed his cap.

"Au-brey." The tinge of frustration crept in again. She'd had this conversation before…with another blond boy. But where? When? She pushed the thought aside. Aubrey turned to look at Warren and noticed that beyond him, Maeve had appeared, walking along with them. Her face, which normally held a contented countenance, had turned critical, her brows pulled together, her eyes slits.

"So, now I know who you are," she continued. "Now, other than not being chaperoned, is there a reason I shouldn't be talking to you?" She asked the question to hear Warren's thoughts, but Aubrey was starting to get ideas of her own as to why she shouldn't be talking to him. The look on Maeve's face was helping form those opinions.

"Look at me, Aubrey." He swept his hand in a broad gesture at himself. "I am the help," he said in a tone that mocked Claire Somerton.

"And I am the guest," Aubrey said trying to separate herself from her hosts, which Warren obviously thought he was beneath. She glanced at Maeve, who was still walking along with them. Aubrey was getting used to Maeve piping in during situations like this, but other than her pinched facial expression, there was nothing being offered.

Aubrey returned her attention to Warren. If this young man knew Maeve, maybe he knew something about her death, Aubrey thought. She needed to keep him talking. For a moment, a memory intruded. She thought of her mother. It was dim, but Aubrey got the feeling she was acting just like her – the part of her she hated the most – the part that conned people out of information, so she could feign her fortune telling routine. She remembered her mother was good at it. Aubrey had seen her play the game a million times and had been embarrassed by it just as many. Well, she would see if she was just as good at it as her mother.

"Where is this beautiful place you're taking me to?" Aubrey asked.

"This way."

She followed him past what she thought was beautiful place after beautiful place, until they passed through a break in a towering hedgerow. "The Hidden Garden," he said. "It was one of – of Maeve's favorite spots."

A finely manicured hedge made a semi-circle that fanned out from a majestic stone wall and patio, like welcoming arms. Aubrey walked through the space toward the wall where water flowed through a massive fountain in its middle. It was an elaborate affair, with water pouring from the head of Bacchus into one main basin. From there, the water flowed through lions' mouths into another stone pool. Carved cherubic toddlers played on the fountain's edges. Aubrey seated herself on one of the stone benches held in place by proud griffins.

"Who are the ladies?" Aubrey asked Warren. Four

marble statues stood equidistant from each other along the surrounding hedgerow.

"The Four Seasons," he replied with reverence.

The garden was quiet other than the lapping flow of water and her own heartbeat and breathing. The beauty, she supposed, lay in the stark contrast between the smooth white marble statuary and the textured rich green of the grass and foliage. Warren had been correct – it formed an unusual beauty.

Aubrey unrolled the pencil pouch. When she looked up again, she noticed Maeve slowly wandering near the hedgerow, hand outstretched as if she were touching the tiny glossy leaves. Harnessing her attention, Aubrey flipped to a blank page in the sketchbook, pausing briefly to note the drawings produced by a living Maeve. Aubrey focused on the griffin closest to her, its feathered wings and its curled mane gathered beneath its chin. As she sketched, she lost track of Warren and was startled when she realized he had seated himself next to her. She felt her heart jump in her chest. It was only because he surprised her, she thought. He leaned to stare over her shoulder, and she became very aware of his chest against her arm. It was warm and strong. Maeve turned from the hedgerow and glared at them, brows knotted and mouth downturned.

"You're even better than Maeve," Warren said.

Aubrey glanced at him. Their eyes met, and he smiled. She felt an unfamiliar spark, and was flooded with warmth. She had never felt like this, not even with Pitch. Time was suspended while her mind flashed with thoughts and images. Warren had said he was Maeve's friend. She was Pitch's friend, too. But this wonderful warmth was different. And it was also impossible. She didn't want it to be, but it was. How important timing was to things, she suddenly thought. If they were in a different time, a different place, there might be a possibility of this being more, but – Aubrey realized she had stopped breathing.

Looking on from the hedgerow, Maeve cleared her throat. Aubrey looked up to see Maeve's eyes slit in anger.

"Did you know her well?" Aubrey asked, looking back to her drawing. As she shaded one of the griffin's feathers, she felt a piece of her hair fall purposely from her twist.

Warren paused too long. Aubrey turned to look at him. He was eyeing her with sudden suspicion.

"Your hair. It's an unusual color at the end. What did you do to it?"

"Oh, that," Aubrey panicked. She dropped the pencil, which rolled off her lap and onto the stones at her feet. She hastily tucked the stray hairs back into the bun to hide their ends the way Maeve had showed her, but it was too late. She glanced up to where Maeve stood. Maeve's eyes were narrowed, and a self-satisfied grin played at one side of her mouth.

"What?" she asked, realizing Warren was still staring at her.

"Who are you, really?"

"What do you mean?" Aubrey fumbled, reaching for

the fallen pencil. "I'm Maeve's friend." She tried to act innocent. Maeve turned away to play with the hedgerow leaves again.

"I never heard Maeve mention you." His tone was accusatory.

"So you were close." It was a statement more than a question. She felt a pang of guilt. For a second she realized she was luring information out of him, playing her mother again. It was at those times that Aubrey could not judge who was more desperate for information – the gullible clients, who sat before Lenora desperate for information on their lost loved ones, or Lenora herself. She despised when her mother took advantage of these people at their weakest moments. Yet at the same moment, she realized she missed her mother. Her mother. She had a life, she suddenly remembered. And this wasn't it. The entire situation overwhelmed her physically. Her stomach churned, and a pain stabbed at her temple.

"What does it matter to you?" An edge had grown in Warren's voice. "Why did you seek me out?"

"I didn't – I was just taking a walk –"

The conversation had turned suddenly tense. Lost in her own thoughts, Aubrey couldn't discern the reason.

"You did. You did seek me out."

"No!"

"With the pretense of sketching."

"But I *am* sketching!" She gestured apologetically to the drawing in front of her. She found she was defending herself, but from what she could not figure.

"Look, I don't know what kind of information Claire Somerton has you fishing for, but you'll get nothing from me. I don't know how her daughter died. I don't know if she was murdered."

Warren rose abruptly and fled down the few steps of the patio area, past Maeve whose eyes sought his. He ran from the Hidden Garden, arms and legs pumping, as if his life depended on it.

Murder.

The idea had been lost to Aubrey amidst all of the lifestyle changes around her. But now she remembered it. Maeve had said it to her that first day. She thought she had been murdered. Supposedly that was why she had pulled Aubrey to this other time – to help her find out about the murder. How Maeve had died and why. And now here it was, blatantly thrown out to her. This young man spoke of murder. Plain and simple. And if Maeve had been murdered, the murderer was still out there.

Aubrey sat alone suffocating in the silence of the Hidden Garden. This was way too much for her. Her thoughts whirled. She couldn't do this. It was ridiculous. It was dangerous. Most days she hid behind her hair in her classes at school, and now the reality hit her – if she could call being in 1912 reality. Maeve intended for her to find her murderer. Aubrey had never done anything like this before, but she assumed that a murderer didn't want to be found, and Aubrey supposed that if he or she knew someone was looking for them, they wouldn't hesitate to murder again.

LENORA SAT IN THE hospital cafeteria at a small round table designed for four. She was alone with her thoughts and a cup of coffee. She spent most of her working life at a table almost like this. A little smaller. And hers was covered with a sapphire tablecloth that brushed the ground with gold bohemian fringe. She gazed into the cardboard cup, much as she would gaze into her crystal ball. People expected a crystal ball, but just like today, it was her own eyes she saw reflected back most often.

Lenora had trained Aubrey from an early age to answer the door when one of her clients called. That way Lenora could have the lights dimmed and be in position. Presentation was everything.

And even though Aubrey was shy, Lenora had trained her to be welcoming and to make polite conversation, which most clients believed was out of earshot.

It was insurance, Lenora justified to her daughter. Purely insurance. She couldn't depend on her gift to be perfectly tuned every day. Sometimes she was off, and a name, a situation, was all a client needed to be satisfied. More often than not, they would return, and many times Lenora found that her gift was more receptive with return customers.

Aubrey participated reluctantly. Lenora had tried to

explain it to her over the years. That often that basic information was a jump start for the mystic conversation her clients expected. That she really did have a gift. She saw things. In daylight. In dreams. Often when she didn't want to. And what she saw often didn't please her and had to be couched carefully to the paying ear.

Lenora's attention moved slowly back to the ebony liquid that had begun to move in small ripples in the cup as she held it in her hands. Her shaking hands. Leonora quickly set the cup down onto the table and moved her hands to her lap. She didn't like what she was seeing now.

Fourteen

THE NEXT MORNING, Aubrey was still shaken with her revelation from the day before. She had barely slept. A murderer lurked here somewhere. Was this person aware yet that she was meant to find him? Did anyone even suspect? Claire hadn't mentioned it and definitely didn't act like her daughter had died any way but naturally. Dalton didn't seem overly concerned either. Warren had been the only one who mentioned it. Was it simply a rumor that had let itself loose among the help?

Aubrey sat nervously on the edge of the bed as Maeve passed slowly back and forth outside the bedroom. Aubrey had attempted to speak to her several times, but Maeve was either ignoring her or couldn't hear her. Aubrey didn't pretend to understand the world Maeve was in. Giving a low, irritated growl, she got up and closed the door as Maeve passed again.

Now it was Aubrey who paced, holding her hands tight as she thought about Maeve's predicament, realizing with growing animosity that it was her predicament as well. She pushed those feelings down. They didn't give her the clarity she needed. Instead, Aubrey thought about those mystery movies and television shows she sometimes watched. As in those cases, she supposed everyone was a suspect. She carefully counted them out on her fingers. Claire, Maeve's own mother. She supposed she'd have to be counted. And Dalton, although she thought he seemed unable to hurt anyone. Then there was Mr. Hadaway. She didn't particularly like him, but that really didn't count for anything. It didn't mean he was a murderer. There were the other servants in the house, but Aubrey hadn't had time to talk with them much. Maybe she should make a point of that, she thought. There were the other workers on the estate, particularly Warren. He said he had hoped Maeve was his friend, and yet, something he had said made her think they had been perhaps closer than that. None of them seemed like murderers. And she was sure there were others who had access to Fairview that she hadn't even met yet.

She sighed, eying the dress laid on the bed. It was getting late.

Mrs. Somerton had provided a white lace tea gown for Aubrey to wear. The three-quarter length sleeves and narrow profile accentuated Aubrey's thin build and long arms. The dress came only to her ankles and showed her tan shoes and their tiny curvy heels. She was getting good at dressing without Maeve's help. But just as she was thinking this, there was a light knock on her door, and the servant girl, Lucy, opened it a crack allowing for just a sliver of her face, so as not to intrude.

"You'll need some help buttoning that up," Lucy said.

"Yes, thank you." Aubrey was starting to realize that she had to accept the servant help – it was expected, both from the people who were her hosts and the servants. The help had been polite and patient, assuming her reluctance stemmed from inexperience with such prosperity.

Lucy smiled sheepishly as she slid surreptitiously into the room. Aubrey turned her back to Lucy, who deftly maneuvered the small pearl buttons through their loops and tied the wide powder pink satin ribbon at Aubrey's waist.

"So what am I to make of this company this afternoon, Lucy?" Aubrey asked.

"There'll be aunts and uncles – and cousins and friends, ma'am," said Lucy, now finished with her work and watching as Aubrey stepped to the mirror to address her hair. "Would you like some help with that?"

"I don't think so, but stay awhile in case, would you?" Aubrey's reflection smiled at Lucy.

"Of course." Lucy stepped back clasping her hands in front of her.

"So there'll be young people?"

"Oh yes," Lucy responded, her eyebrows showing excitement. "They always seem to enjoy themselves. Dinner will be served, and they're already setting up for a croquet tournament on the front lawn."

"Croquet? I don't think I've ever really played croquet." First solve a murder and now play croquet? She wasn't sure which one she felt least able to do. In her hesitation at this thought, the hairs began to slip from the twist she was attempting. Lucy stepped in, fastening the knot with pins as Aubrey held it.

"You're a vision, miss," Lucy commented, unsolicited. "If you don't know how to play croquet, you won't have to worry. There'll be plenty of young men who will be falling over themselves to teach you!"

"Why, thank you Lucy," Aubrey said out of politeness. She blushed as she spoke. Boys didn't usually pay her any attention. Except for Pitch, and he was just a friend. But then again, she hardly recognized the girl in the mirror.

Fifteen

A S THE CARRIAGES and cars started arriving, Aubrey saw why Mrs. Somerton had insisted she wear the white tea dress. All of the women were wearing variations of it.

It was apparently the newest style. Even the older women wore white lace, although many of their dresses had bustles or they carried parasols. The older women wore elaborate hats, too, either flat-topped and surrounded with flowers, or pluming up above their heads with feathers and veiling. Men were outfitted with suits and vests. Some wore flat-topped straw hats and carried walking sticks. Even on this hot afternoon, at this casual gathering, all were the height of fashion. They chattered as they arrived, hugging and shaking hands as their horses and carriages were led away.

Claire emerged from Fairview onto the stone veranda under the carriage port. She was dressed in a pink tea-length dress trimmed with lace and draped with a flowing fabric that was caught with small wreaths of flowers at a pale blue ribbon that wrapped her waist. The small wreaths of flowers also caught the fabric at several places on the skirt. Another wide ribbon was tied over her hair like a headband and allowed her golden curls to frame a face that emitted an easy warmth, which was returned by her guests. Faces and hugs were momentarily somber as relatives and friends inquired about Claire's wellbeing since Maeve's passing. But creased brows were soon replaced by understanding nods. Claire smiled graciously through it all, as did Maeve, who had glided behind her. The young girl resembled her mother, Aubrey noticed. And she was positively glowing with excitement.

Many who arrived treated the property as if it were their own home, one they had been away from for a while and were pleased to see again. Some entered the house proper with sighs of satisfaction that can only come from a sense of comfort, while others strode around the verandas, thumbs in their vest pockets to gaze on the gardens, which gleamed like gems in the afternoon sun.

"Aubrey, dear," Claire held out her hand beckoning Aubrey toward her as she greeted one group of young guests. Maeve circled the group as if trying to be noticed by the popular crowd. "Aubrey, this is Maeve's cousin, Taj. Taj, dear, this is Aubrey, Maeve's school friend who has come to visit. Would you be so kind as to make sure she meets the others?" Even though it was spoken as a request, the task was understood.

"We've been friends since childhood," Maeve blurted childishly in Aubrey's direction. Aubrey did her best to ignore her, but Maeve's unpredictable moods kept her on edge.

"Of course Aunt Claire," the young man replied. He was tall, his thin stature emphasized by his slim pants, vest and coat. "My name is Taj Somerton," he said with a smile punctuated by deep dimples. Aubrey blushed before he took her hand, and bowing, brushed it with his lips. "The pleasure is all mine! Looks like we'll have a fine tournament this afternoon!"

"Oh I do wish I could play!" Maeve interjected. "Taj always was my favorite partner."

Aubrey dipped her head to hide an eye roll, regretted it immediately, and hoped it came off as coy. She followed Taj's gaze toward the green expanse of lawn where the help was turning the grounds into a sight fit for a festival. Final efforts were being made to string ribbons between short posts that had been hammered into the ground to outline the croquet courts. There were at least six courts in the open areas of the lawn, each outlined with a different color. They had been strategically located so that an edge or two of each court were shaded by nearby trees. Servants had already moved benches, wicker chairs and small tables beneath the overhanging branches near the courts so that players could relax as they awaited their turn. Tables were trimmed with bright cloths, and more servants were already loading them with pitchers of lemonade, iced teas and sparkling glasses. Tiered serving dishes laden with sweets and finger sandwiches were carefully being set into place.

Aubrey looked back to the house, seeking and finding Claire. She was there, standing alone near an urn filled with flowers while the garden party blossomed around her. What a peculiar woman, Aubrey mused. The look on Claire's face was a mixture of sadness and regret, yet her posture was one of elegance and duty. Surely, she was thinking of Maeve –

"We'll need players for our first round." Taj's words interrupted her thoughts. He scanned the crowd. "Ah, Missy! Emmet!" he hollered. "We'll take you on!"

"Oh, yes, Taj! They'll make for a jolly first round!" Maeve squealed to his unhearing ears.

Maeve's enthusiasm for an event that she would only be able to view from the sidelines, and her determination to insert herself into the conversation, was beginning to eat at Aubrey's focus. She again tried to follow Taj's searching eyes.

A young woman, stunning in her lace tea dress and a large white hat, looked up at the sound of her name and smiled in their direction. A young man with her, probably Emmet, Aubrey deduced, led her by the elbow, each carrying their mallets. They looked like confident competitors. Aubrey felt herself being more and more concerned with her ability to pull this off.

"Oh, I'll just watch –" Aubrey tried to interject.

"Nonsense," Taj said, fanning her words away.

"But I've never really learned to play –"

"I play very well," Maeve reminded everyone and no

one.

"What? Never played?" Taj acknowledged Aubrey's dismay, but continued to scan the crowd. "Well, never you mind. You'll learn as we go. I can tell you're a fast study. You'll pick it up in no time. Now, we need two more players –"

Taj lifted his head to peruse the crowd. "Ah, there's Suzanne and Joshua – Joshua!" he called.

Over the heads of the other guests, Aubrey could see the young man's eyes crease in a grin before he consulted the young lady next to him. Aubrey could see her smile as she bobbed her head in an effort to see Taj. Their eagerness was palpable, Aubrey noticed.

"Oh, two more good choices, Taj," Maeve said.

When the new couple reached them, there was hugging and back slapping and hand shaking.

"And this is Aubrey, Maeve's friend from Brayden," Taj said with acceptance and approval in his voice. And because it was Taj who said it, Aubrey got the distinct impression everyone was to see it that way.

There were smiles all around, and the newest young lady to join them, Suzanne, cupped Aubrey's hand in hers and said with a charm that warmed her, "We are so pleased to meet you, Aubrey. We really are sorry about the family's loss – yours as well." Her smile faded briefly. "Maeve loved these parties…"

Maeve's glee faded at the past tense of her existence. Aubrey met Maeve's eyes and held them before turning her full attention to Suzanne.

"Yes, Maeve spoke fondly of them," Aubrey said

earnestly, remembering Maeve's first conversation with her in the Japanese Garden. It felt good to be saying something she knew to be true instead of the fabrications that seemed to be coming out of her mouth so often lately. Maeve smiled a small "thank you," but her eyes remained full of loss. She glided a short distance away, but kept listening.

Suzanne leaned in as if to relay her best kept secret. "Claire's not one to cancel any gathering, and this one has been on the calendar since last year. But *I* think she is also using it to hide her grief." Suzanne raised her eyebrows and nodded to emphasize her opinion's probability of correctness.

"Suzanne! You're already monopolizing Aubrey!" Taj's attentions made Aubrey blush again. "I'll have you know she's keeping me company today! Now, are we going to play croquet, or are we going to stand around and gossip?"

Sixteen

AUBREY FELT A tiny electrical current run through her as Taj placed his hand on her lower back and steered her toward the court outlined in blue ribbon.

He selected a mallet and handed it to her.

"Here, take this one. You'll follow me, and don't worry. Pay attention to what the others are doing and no one will be the wiser!" He whispered his directions and grinned mischievously. "It will be our secret!"

Joshua started the game by smacking a wooden ball through the first two hoops, and Aubrey noticed that Suzanne did the same. But when the court became littered with five balls and it was her turn, she began to panic. Her anxiety was apparently clear on her face because Taj gently prodded her toward the start of the court, flashing his dimples.

"Don't worry about the others," he said. "Just concentrate on those first two hoops."

Aubrey felt her cheeks turning red as she willed herself to have confidence. She had never been one for sports, especially not dressed like this. She wacked the ball and it flew cleanly through the hoops. Aubrey smiled at Taj, pleased with herself, and he smiled back nodding toward the next hoop, eyebrows raised in encouragement. She struck the ball again but missed the hoop.

"You have one more turn, Aubrey! Get it around the right side!"

She set it up for what she assumed would be her next turn, but by the time the five players had taken their numerous hits – with free shots she couldn't figure out how they earned – she was lost. The easy part was remembering what hoops she was supposed to hit her ball through next. The difficult part was actually doing that while others knocked her out of the way. Gradually, thanks to Taj's carefree nature and gentle cajoling, Aubrey was able to relax enough that she found herself laughing at her own mistakes and Emmett's lame jokes.

"Taj is such an unusual name," Aubrey said trying to make small talk while they sipped lemonade and waited their turns.

"Oh it's just a nick name," he said. "My real name is Andrew. When I was younger, my parents took me on a six-month trip through Asia. We saw the Taj Mahal, and apparently I couldn't stop talking about it. Drove everyone mad, although I don't remember any of it. Ever since then, everyone has called me Taj."

Suddenly Missy cheered, raising her mallet triumphantly.

"Ah, blast!" Taj proclaimed at Missy's win. "Seems we're out of it, Sweet Aubrey. We put up a gallant fight though!"

They all laughed at his dramatics, but Aubrey realized her showing had been disastrous.

"Let us retire our mallets. Would you care for a stroll?"

"Don't let me keep you from the other guests," Aubrey said as he took her mallet from her. She noticed Missy and Emmet walking off to find out where their next round would be played, and the others were moving in the direction of refreshments. "You have been polite enough to endure my pathetic attempts at croquet!"

"The other guests pale in comparison to your company," he persuaded.

"I know Claire intended for you all to keep me company, but really, I can manage this crowd on my own."

"So you are casting me off?" he said, his eyes suddenly round with faux distress. Aubrey laughed at his playfulness.

"Oh, Taj, how guilty you make me feel. All right! You've worn me down!"

He leaned their mallets against a nearby tree trunk and, putting a gentle hand on her elbow, led her across the lawn toward the gardens while weaving their way around groups sitting and talking at small tables and youngsters playing tag around trees.

"So, are you enjoying your time here at Fairview?"

"Oh, yes. Mrs. Somerton has been so kind to me."

"That's right, you were supposed to be summering with Maeve, weren't you?"

"Yes."

"That must be a bit uncomfortable for you. Are arrangements being made for you to return home?"

"Uh…yes."

He turned to look at her.

"I mean, I don't mind being here. I am starting to appreciate just how much Maeve loved it here. You think you know someone. I knew her at school," she lied, "but now, I'm seeing how it must have been here for her –"

"Yes, I can see that." Taj contemplated the grounds, soaking in the dazzling vistas in every direction.

They walked in silence for a bit. Although it was not an altogether uncomfortable silence, Aubrey looked for another topic.

"That building up ahead. I haven't gotten to ask anyone about it yet."

"The aviary? Surely you've heard about Claire's bird collection."

"No, actually, I haven't."

"Let's go look." His smile spread across his face, and he stepped up his pace as they crossed a drive.

The building they approached reminded Aubrey of another building she had seen once, but she couldn't remember where. It seemed years ago. That building, a pale shadow in her memory, had been part of a garden, she thought she recalled. This one, although it too looked like a castle with parapets and arched windows, was not as rough-hewn. She let the memory fade and focused on the structure in front of her. This one had an enormous cage off the back of it. Rectangular at first, it ended in a round, domed affair. Aubrey estimated that the top of the rectangular cage was at least fifteen feet above the ground. The domed portion had to be at least thirty feet high, she estimated. He saw the awe on her face.

"Quite fantastic, isn't it?" She nodded in stunned silence, so he continued. "This is only one of several buildings. Aunt Claire has the largest private aviary in the country. I can't even begin to tell you the variety that exists in there – plovers and magpies and parrots. And you need to look closely. There are different shaped tails, and different colored beaks. She has them shipped in from all over the world." He seemed frustrated at his inability to impress upon her the variety so that she could fully appreciate it. "And then there is her fascination with peacocks. That is what the building up front is primarily for – the peacocks and the tumbling pigeons."

"Tumbling pigeons?"

He grinned. "You think I'm pulling your leg, don't you? Maybe we'll be able to spot them."

Aubrey was only temporarily distracted by the idea of tumbling pigeons, be they real or not. It was the other bird he had mentioned that brought back a distant memory – that one, too, stretching back, so far back, it seemed.

"She has peacocks, too?"

"Yes, here they come! They must think we're going to feed them."

Several peacocks picked their way carefully toward them across the yard of the cage. While most of them wore the brilliant iridescent blues and greens of Indian peacocks, two were pure white, trailing tails that looked as if they were made of lace. Her brain fought for a moment. A hand reached out to pet a similar creature, but someone shouted and the hand quickly retracted.

"I've never seen albino peacocks," Aubrey said, pushing the vision aside.

"Oh, they're not albino," he said. "They are white. If they were albino, their eyes would be red."

Aubrey nodded her understanding.

"Claire originally purchased them for Maeve," Taj continued. "I remember hearing about the day the birds arrived. They came in crates by train, and when they arrived here at Fairview, Maeve rushed to meet them. Maeve was smitten from the start, they say. And that day, when the workers saw the birds dragging their tails like the train of a wedding gown and Maeve's white lace dress, they couldn't help but make the comparison."

Aubrey smiled at the image.

"Maeve took to the creatures quite uncannily – and they to her," he added. "One peacock would eat out of her hand. But then, it was found dead in the cage, its neck snapped."

Aubrey stopped short.

"Someone killed it?"

"No one ever confirmed that. I remember someone

saying that it could have flown into the cage and broken its neck –"

"That seems unlikely," Aubrey countered.

"They say it happens, though." Taj tipped his head and raised a brow, secretly agreeing with her skepticism.

Seventeen

TAJ NODDED soberly. "They never found out who – if anyone – killed the peacock. Claire was sure it was a disturbed worker, but no one was able to figure it out. Maeve was devastated. She had just lost her father and then the bird. She was so devastated that Claire had the creature stuffed. Surely you've seen it?"

"Actually no, I don't think I have," Aubrey said, although she was still plagued by the distant vision of a stuffed white bird.

"Maeve insisted her mother keep it in the library – that was Maeve's favorite room. She wanted to have it near her, but she may not have kept it there after Maeve's death. I think Aunt Claire is trying desperately to remove unpleasant reminders."

Aubrey thought about this. It was all new information. The peacocks were at the wall of the enclosure looking at her expectantly. She squatted down for a closer look.

They were beautiful birds, elegant with their tails draping behind them – like the train of a lace dress. Another image seemed to flash through Aubrey's mind, but she couldn't hang on to it. The bird cocked its head, the little bobbly crown feathers dancing as it did so. Its eye blinked at her. Again, a fleeting image ricocheted through her brain. Too fast. Too fast, she thought. She put a hand to her forehead. If only she could hang on to the image longer. She was sure it was important.

"Are you all right?" Taj's voice broke through. "I didn't mean to upset you."

"No, no, I'm fine," Aubrey stammered. "Just a bit of a headache."

She stood up, smoothed her skirt and swallowed her nagging discomfort. "How, exactly does one go about getting an animal stuffed?"

"The Somertons are lucky. Mr. Brighton is also a taxidermist."

"Mr. Brighton? I don't think I've met him."

"No? They're old friends, or at least he was friends with Uncle Edgar. Taught him all the ins and outs of taxidermy. For Uncle Edgar it was a kind of hobby. Haven't you noticed all the displays around Fairview?"

"Oh." The vision of the cavernous main hall with its heads, pelts, and birds came to mind. She hadn't thought it was any different from any other mansion of its time, but apparently it was.

"Come on, I'll show you." Aubrey expected Taj to take her back toward Fairview, but he gently took her arm again and started them on a walk away from the main buildings.

"Now, Mr. Brighton helps Aunt Claire with her aviary," he said as they walked. "He makes recommendations to her, does the purchasing, instructs her on care for the birds. He's actually the director of the state zoo, but he spends many weeks here. He uses Uncle Edgar's old workshop to work in."

"And he's the one who stuffed Maeve's peacock?"

"Yes, took him quite a while, but Maeve was pleased. She'd stand there petting the thing and talking to it like it was alive. Bertie, she called him."

They had arrived at a collection of smaller, rough wooden buildings that resembled large sheds.

He opened the door to one of them, and Aubrey gasped. The dark interior was hung round with a ghastly display of pelts, skulls, plaster casts of headless animals, and bones of all sorts and sizes. A work table was littered with string, clay scrapings, assorted small tools, and jars of small glass discs. Along one wall sat a metal tub, empty but emanating a strong chemical smell.

"I seemed to have distressed you again," Taj said, his face fallen.

"Oh, no – no." Aubrey tried to relieve him of the guilt she heard in his voice. Claire had entrusted him with entertaining her, and she was sure he felt he was failing at his duty. "The shadows and – skulls – and such just startled me."

"How thoughtless of me. This place is too gruesome for a lady – especially after your best friend's passing."

"No really, Taj. I'm all right now. It's really very

fascinating – the smell is just strong."

He offered her a handkerchief, and she held it to her mouth and nose. The cloth, smelling of a manly spiciness, seemed to help her stand the strong odor of the shed.

"I don't know much about it, but I believe the chemicals preserve the skin against aging and insects. Mr. Brighton taught Uncle Edgar so much. Mr. Brighton has done quite a bit of experimenting with his own mixture of chemicals, which are expected to extend the life of the specimen. He believes the animal should be posed as it would be seen in its habitat, and so sometimes he adds beautifully painted backgrounds or other animals that would be in the habitat. He's really a fascinating man to talk to."

"Seems that he would be. But Maeve was only interested in Bertie?"

"Yes, I suppose so. While her father was alive, she might have joined him here during the finishing work, but she could never have stood the sk—," Taj caught himself. "The beginning steps. How you do make me forget myself, Aubrey."

Forget myself.

Taj's words stopped her as so many other things had today. The words seemed innocent enough. Just a saying. But for a second they seemed more than that. There seemed to be another half memory in there somewhere, at the edge of Aubrey's awareness. She put her hand to her head again.

Forget myself.

Aubrey couldn't help thinking she was beginning to forget her own self. Whatever that meant.

Eighteen

THAT NIGHT, as Aubrey sat at the dressing table in her room and pulled the pins from her hair, she stared at her reflection lost in thought. Maeve's father, Edgar, had died a little more than a year ago. Someone had broken the neck of a beautiful, innocent peacock. Then Maeve had died after a quiet dinner with her mother. Then, just the other day, that boy who worked on the gardens.

It seemed like so many deaths in one place in the span of a year. Were that many deaths coincidental? But if they were related, how?

Warren had mentioned murder.

Maeve had used that word on their first meeting. And just the other day, Warren used it. Were others on the estate thinking the same thing? Aubrey tapped the hairpin she was holding on the table's top. If murder were the case, who could be responsible?

She had read her share of mystery novels. There always had to be a motive.

Claire Somerton seemed to waffle between a moody, self-absorbed business woman and a cheerful hostess, neither trait of which called to mind a woman who had just lost her only child.

But grief could take different faces for different people, Aubrey tried to rationalize. She played with the lid of a small trinket box on the dressing table while her thoughts swirled. What would Claire gain by offing her own daughter?

There was Dalton. Surely not him. He had befriended her almost immediately upon her arrival. But Aubrey recalled his almost too friendly attitude toward Claire, supposedly the wife of his best friend. Perhaps he had something to gain with the daughter out of the way. Had there been a love triangle, or would it maybe change who inherited the estate?

What about Frank Hadaway, Claire's project supervisor? He was a world-famous landscape architect. Young. Well on his way. Surely, he didn't need to kill a teenager to obtain fortune and fame.

What was that taxidermy guy's name? Aubrey frantically tapped the hairpin, trying to jog her memory. Brighton – that was it. He had everything going for him, too. Director of the state zoo, a world-renowned naturalist. How could murder be in his best interest?

Thinking about it, Aubrey was getting the impression Warren had feelings for Maeve. Surely, it hadn't been him.

But there were so many others on the estate, not to mention all the others who visited on a regular basis. Any of them could be responsible, if it had been murder. There had been no investigation – the household had treated it as a death by natural causes. Aubrey was supposedly a visiting friend – a teenager, a girl – no one would tell her anything of any significance, even if she asked. And she was quickly realizing she had no business asking. Maeve had given her an impossible task.

Aubrey slapped a hairpin down on the dressing table with more force than she intended.

This wasn't her problem. It was dead and gone – more than a hundred years dead and gone.

This wasn't her life. Aubrey stared at her reflection in the mirror – was it? There she sat, her dark hair falling around her face. The burgundy tips of her hair fading away. Hand-made white lace encircled her throat. She glimpsed what she once would have called antique furniture in the reflected background. But it wasn't antique here. It was modern.

Where was she supposed to be? Too many things were blurring. She missed her home, and yet she fought to remember it.

In the background of the reflection, another figure began to materialize. Maeve stepped out of a fog and gradually came into focus behind her. She sat casually on the bed as if she lived there.

Nineteen

"WELL, HOW is our enterprise proceeding?" Maeve's voice was critical, her visage stony. She smoothed her skirt as she sat, much like Aubrey had seen Claire Somerton do.

"I've been talking with everyone, as you know. Trying to keep a low profile…" Aubrey's reflection spoke to Maeve.

Maeve raised a critical eyebrow.

"Hoping no one will suspect what I am up to," Aubrey explained.

"Ah," Maeve said, although not sounding quite convinced. She returned to fingering the lace on her skirt.

"I've listened to a lot of conversations, and I've been trying to put the pieces together." Aubrey had still not turned from the vanity mirror and spoke to Maeve's reflection.

"Thank you," Maeve said. Aubrey couldn't help

question the sincerity in the comment. "Have you discovered if I was murdered? *Why* I was murdered?"

"You know," Aubrey hesitated. "This is difficult." She paused, assessing Maeve. "It's not like you are an impartial third party." Maeve raised her brow.

"A relative or something," Aubrey clarified. "What are you going to do with this information once I give it to you? How will this change things? You'll still be –" Aubrey sought for tactful words. "You'll still be like this."

"I don't know how it will change things," Maeve said, looking down.

Aubrey turned on the vanity bench and faced Maeve.

"I want to go back," Aubrey said defiantly.

"You can't. Not yet," Maeve shot back, less breathy than usual.

"Why not?" Aubrey countered sharply. Quietly, she added, "I miss my mother. At least I think I do." She couldn't quite remember, but she was sure she had a mother.

"I miss my mother too – and my father," Maeve added after a moment.

"Isn't he – with you somewhere?" Aubrey was confused. "I mean he's –"

Maeve became oddly distant. She stared away as she spoke. "He's here. I see my father. He's nearby. I know he is. I can see him through that fog, but I can't get to him. It's as if he can't see me, can't hear me." Her gaze returned to Aubrey, and it was imploring. "Remember I said there were things I could do, but there were a lot of things I couldn't do?"

"Yes."

"Well, often, I'll see him. Right on the other side of something, maybe a hedge. He'll be looking away from me, doing something. Maybe bending over, looking at a blossom. And I'll call to him, 'Father! Father!' But he won't stop what he's doing. He won't even flinch, won't even show that maybe he's heard me but doesn't want to look. I'll call again, 'Father?' But he'll give me no response. I'll try to go to him. To touch his arm or something to get his attention," she hesitated. "But I won't be able to get to him. Something stops me."

"Is there like a barrier or something?" Aubrey asked, trying to understand.

"No, not a physical barrier. It's more as if something is just preventing me. I can't move to him." She put her face in her hands and spoke into them.

"There are so many things here that I don't understand, and there's no one to help me understand. I guess I'm just hoping that if I can fill in the gaps, it will get me closer to my father. His company here would be so…welcome. I miss him so. I miss everybody."

Aubrey understood missing everyone. She had just assumed since Maeve was a ghost she would automatically be with her father. She didn't understand this other world and was surprised that although Maeve was a part of it, she didn't understand it either.

"You think knowing who did this to you would change things?"

Maeve sniffled daintily and looked at Aubrey. "I

don't know. I was hoping so."

"I just don't know how much more I can do, Maeve," she said in frustration. "People here know I'm a stranger. They have no reason to trust me, to take me into their confidence – and I can't be here long enough to win their trust. I've done my best. You're going to have to be content with that."

"No. I can't go on like this – not knowing – forever."

Forever. It was a word Aubrey and her friends threw around all the time. But Maeve really meant it. Forever.

Twenty

AUBREY LAY in bed the next morning, knowing she would be late for breakfast with Claire and the rest of the adults. She had been up most of the night, tossing and turning, weighing people's prospective motives, and trying to figure out how to proceed.

Last night she had turned back to the vanity mirror, to this reflection of a life. Maeve's pain was becoming her pain. She felt it in her stomach. A gut wrenching nausea.

This morning, that nausea still haunted her. Perhaps breakfast would help. Just a light quick one, then she could feign a walk in the gardens but really go off to investigate....

Investigate – that seemed like a bizarre word to be using. She was fifteen. She didn't investigate things. She shook off that notion. Maybe the old Aubrey didn't investigate, but she *had* to now. It seemed like the only way.

But where to start? She'd have to start thinking like a detective. She had only been playing at it. Forgetting why she was here. Enjoying the food, the gardens and – Taj. His bright eyes and engaging smile. The way he took her elbow and escorted her along the walkways. Even Warren was handsome and charming – although a bit complex. If she wasn't sure Claire would try to send her home soon, she could have stayed here forever. Forever. Maeve's pain and loneliness surfaced again in her thoughts. This was a wonderful place. No wonder Maeve was so lonesome.

So where to start? She plopped her arms above her head, stretching them on the pillow. She stared at the ceiling, thinking again of the – it seemed so odd to use the word – suspects.

Of all the people that she had met so far, Frank Hadaway seemed the most suspicious. Her brow creased in thought. Although she couldn't quite decide how killing a young girl would help out a man already on his way to international fame and fortune, she hadn't liked his attitude and demeanor since she met him at that first supper. So how did one investigate someone? How did someone find out about how and why that person did the things they did? She had listened to his conversation at the breakfast table. He had seemed too casual, almost flip and insulting when he engaged Claire in conversation. Claire had cut him short and so had Dalton. But why had he acted that way? Claire was giving him the opportunity of a lifetime, it would seem, designing so many beautiful gardens. Aubrey wondered how many projects like this he had done before. Was this early in his career or later? He seemed young.

Aubrey sighed and pulled herself up in the bed propping herself among the pillows and against the headboard. She would go down to breakfast. Maybe he would be there. She could listen for more clues, maybe ask some questions.

There was a knock on the door. "Miss Aubrey, are you awake?"

She recognized Lucy's voice.

"Yes, Lucy, you may come in." The maid poked her head into the room.

"Mrs. Somerton just wondered if you were coming to breakfast or if they should start without you."

"Oh, my! I didn't think they'd wait for me!" She jumped out of bed. Lucy was already at the closet pulling out a day dress. Aubrey slipped out of her night clothes and into the dress as Lucy held it for her. As she made her way down the grand staircase, Aubrey realized she was also seriously slipping into her new role.

Knives and forks were already singing their morning song on the fine china. Night woes and daily plans were being discussed by the time Aubrey arrived at the table.

"Aubrey, dear, I hope the festivities yesterday weren't too much for you," Dalton said between chews.

"I am so sorry I'm late," Aubrey said as she placed her napkin on her lap. "I didn't think you'd wait for me. I guess I slept late and then the birds were just singing so beautifully outside my window that I'm afraid I just laid there enjoying it. The minutes must have gotten away from me."

Claire's teacup had paused at her lips.

"I didn't realize you liked nature so much," Mrs. Somerton said, sipping her tea and replacing the cup in the saucer.

"But of course she must if she enjoys sketching," Mr. Hadaway said. "I hope you are finding some suitable scenes in the gardens?"

It was the first time Mr. Hadaway had addressed Aubrey directly. Her mind raced to keep him engaged in conversation – one that could provide her with some insights.

"The gardens are lovely. Just yesterday I began sketching some of the statuary in the Hidden Garden," she said.

"Hmmm… Maeve's favorite," her mother said.

"Yes, it was," Mr. Hadaway said. "Surprisingly enough."

"Why do you say that, Mr. Hadaway?" Aubrey leaped at the chance to get into his mind.

"It wasn't meant to be a child's garden. But then again, Maeve wasn't really a child anymore." There was a gleam in his eye. Mrs. Somerton made a noise from her throat that sounded like disgust.

"Well, he's right, Claire. She wasn't," Dalton said.

"It's a moot point," Claire said. Pushing her plate away, she made to leave the table.

Dang. Aubrey frowned. It was happening again. They

were talking in some sort of code, and the conversation was drifting from where she needed it to be.

"Why isn't it a child's garden, Mr. Hadaway?" Aubrey said in the politest voice she could muster. She noticed that although Mr. Hadaway turned toward her, he still watched Claire out of the corner of his eye. Claire pushed in her chair and drifted toward The Bower doors, removing herself from the conversation.

Mr. Hadaway pulled his gaze from Claire, and focused on Aubrey. "It is meant to be an adult garden. A quiet, meditative spot," he said. "A child wouldn't see the beauty in its simplicity."

"But Maeve did," Claire said, more to herself than to the people in the room as she stared outside.

"Yes, Claire, she did." It was Dalton who acknowledged her spoken thought.

"It was one of the things I loved about her," she whispered. Her hand found the door casing and she leaned into the frame.

"Yes, I as well." It was Mr. Hadaway who said it. Claire turned her head and cast what Aubrey thought was a glare. "She was much more attune to mature musings," he added, fumbling.

Claire turned back to the glass doors. A pause as heavy as a pending thunderstorm gathered in the room.

"Ah-hem." Dalton cleared his throat in an attempt to clear the air. "So, Frank, what do you have planned for this morning?"

"We're still working on the Rock Garden. Laying the canyons. That should soon be finishing up. And I have a team putting final touches on the garden house above."

Aubrey watched Claire cast another icy glare over her shoulder. Why did the garden house cause her to have such an intense reaction?

"Ah, yes," Dalton worked to rein in the storm clouds. "Claire, what about you? Is there any way I can be of assistance this morning?"

"I have some accounts to see to. Some purchases we could discuss," she said, her gaze again directed outside.

"Good. Good. And you, Aubrey? What plans have you today?"

"The day is so beautiful. I might finish those sketches I told you about."

"A wonderful plan. Such a beautiful day. I'll ask the staff to serve a light lunch in The Bower, if that's all right with you Claire."

"It's fine, although I might take mine in my office today."

"Whatever suits you," Dalton said.

"Claire, I'd be honored if you'd come down to check on the progress of your newest garden," Mr. Hadaway said, as he rose and pushed in his chair.

"I have every intention, Mr. Hadaway," she said turning.

"Claire, I didn't mean to offend," he added. "The garden house I planned for –"

Aubrey noticed that with the mention of the garden house, Claire's eyes again narrowed with a steeliness. "You needn't remind me," Claire said.

"Well, it's almost finished. My hope is that now you

can enjoy it. A sanctuary for your soul."

Claire made that noise again, the one edged with disgust. "I'll be in my office, Dalton," she said, as she left the room and headed down the hall to her office in the rear of the house.

"I'll be in the Rock Garden if you need me, Dalton," Mr. Hadaway said pretentiously, and he departed through the hall to the front of the house. Dalton turned to look at Aubrey, who remained seated at the table with him.

"Ah, yes," Aubrey said, folding her napkin. "I'm going to get my sketching supplies, and then I'll be on my way as well." Another plan was brewing in the back of her mind.

Twenty-one

AUBREY LEFT the house with the full intention of finding a place to sketch. She walked the path along the Deer Park toward the Hidden Garden by way of the Japanese Garden. But as she walked along the Deer Park, it was as if something began to possess her. Her mind churned. Up to this point, her attempts at gathering information had been ineffectual. She was going to have to take some risks if she wanted answers. Aubrey spotted Mr. Hadaway's cottage among a stand of maples, and her feet took on a will of their own. She glanced nervously over her shoulders, and sure no one was nearby, cut along the edge of the trees and into their midst.

Her shoes, or rather Maeve's shoes, made hardly a sound on the soft earth, where just enough sunshine urged the grass to grow. Her skin tingled with apprehension as she tried the first wooden step to the porch. It creaked, and she looked nervously over her shoulder. Only Maeve stood among the trees. She nodded her encouragement. Aubrey decided she should look as if she had business with Mr. Hadaway. She gathered her skirt in her hand and mounted the steps, her head held high with purpose. She rapped sharply on the door. The silence she expected greeted her, but acting as if someone were there, she smiled and opened the screen door and then the wooden one.

As she slipped into the narrow front room, Aubrey realized she had forgotten to breathe. Closing her eyes, she drew air into her nearly collapsed lungs. What on earth was she doing? With her hand still on the doorknob behind her, she leaned against the door, encouraging it to close. She swallowed and opened her eyes.

The front room in which she stood appeared to serve as Hadaway's office. His most important papers would be here, she reasoned. But where to start. A rectangular table occupied the center of the room with two chairs drawn up to it. It was covered with a scattering of enormous sheets of paper covered with drawings and sketches. This was where Hadaway drew up his plans and met with clients, she reasoned. Book shelves lined the opposite wall. Books were arranged neatly, but here and there, papers were piled among them. She drifted toward them and fingered through them, lifting their edges now and then to peer at their contents. She didn't know what she was looking for, but these looked like business papers and old ledgers. She drifted toward a secretary that stood to the right with its writing area open. More ledgers. She opened one and studied dates along the margin. Recent dates. But what she thought would be plant names or worker names and payments, was more a listing of tasks completed and to-do lists. This, she thought, might yield some insight into his plans.

Aubrey pulled a high stool up to the desk and began thumbing through the thin book. Hadaway's writing was difficult to read, but here and there she found phrases that made sense, phrases that described the progress of the gardens.

"Takamura will be consulted about authenticity of tea house. Letter sent."

"Bronze Buddha to arrive within two weeks. Have crew at depot."

"Cedars need to be moved to flank tori gate. Gave warning they would outgrow space within two years."

It was the last entry, written months ago when the Japanese garden was being constructed, that caught Aubrey's eye. *Gave warning*? To whom?

She ran her finger down the page, looking for other similar comments. Something other than the day-to-day to-do list for the landscape architect.

Now that she had a focus, the odd comments began to pop out throughout the log. She flipped pages, running her finger down the entries.

"Says this is what she wants."

"I maintain it is a poor choice for the lighting there."

"…against my wishes."

Aubrey's finger stopped on the page. "Where is the

full control I was told I would have? Something must be done."

Something must be done? Was there enough in that thought to warrant her suspicion? Surely Hadaway was talking about Mrs. Somerton. But would he have killed Maeve over a few plant choices? As she pondered this new information, Aubrey lifted her head from the books. Her eyes wandered over the room and locked with horror on the front door – and a figure standing there.

It was Hadaway.

He slammed the door with such force the glass in the windows shook against their frames.

"Why you little wretch!"

Aubrey stumbled backwards without fully standing, knocking over the stool on which she had been sitting.

"How dare you?" Mr. Hadaway's eyes shot fire at Aubrey.

He was advancing on her, backing her against the wall. "I... I was merely looking for a piece of paper to leave you a note," Aubrey stammered, but even she could hear the guilt in her voice.

"A note, eh? And what did you need to tell me?" He was close to her now. She could smell his breath. "You knew I wasn't going to be here. You knew I was going to the construction site." His voice was accusatory. His tone, his closeness – he was scaring her.

"I wanted to ask you a question about Maeve." She looked around him, trying to gauge her chances of getting to the door.

"Maeve?"

"Yes, I never seem to be able to ask any… private questions… at the table."

He backed off slightly, but only slightly.

Aubrey saw her chance. She pushed him aside and made a run for the door.

But he was young and quick. He made a grab for her skirts and caught the fabric. She heard a rip, but not before he had grabbed her hair. Her head was jerked back. She fought the urge to cry, but tears flowed automatically from the pain in her temples and scalp.

"You're hurting me!" she managed.

Ignoring her pleas, he grabbed hold of her wrist and twisted it up and behind her back, wrenching her shoulder. He had spun her away from the front door and was forcing her through another doorway into the inner rooms of the cottage.

"Maeve," he grunted. At first she thought that in his insanity he was mistaking her for Claire's daughter. Then she realized it was a delayed response to her pathetic invention of wanting to ask him a private question about Maeve. "I almost had Claire's permission," he rambled.

She slowly realized the name she had tossed at him had struck a chord. She tried to wriggle free, but he had a firm hold and marched her through to the kitchen.

"Permission?" she managed through the pain. *Keep him talking,* she thought. *Keep him distracted.*

He reached around her and flung open the back door. She stumbled down the back steps, but her feet weren't really necessary. They dangled just above the wood as he held her up by her hair.

"I could have married into this family," he said.

Only half hearing his comment, Aubrey glanced wildly around. There was no one, probably no one even close enough to hear a scream. And that would only further infuriate him.

"Keep walking!" He shoved her forward. She kept her eyes moving as best she could, hoping someone would see them, realize she was in trouble.

"You…loved her?" she managed through the pain. *Just keep him talking.*

"*Her*? Silly girl! I love *this place*!" He pushed her quickly along, across the small lawn, through a thicket of trees to a dirt access road. She only glimpsed the short journey through eyes shuttered to the pain.

"This place is the crowning jewel of my life." They were approaching a large shed. She squinted at it through the pain. She knew this place. She had been here before.

"To sculpt these gardens –" He let go of her hair, and with his free hand quickly dug keys from his pocket and unlocked the padlock on the door. " – and then let them go?"

He opened the door and shoved her inside. She tripped on something and fell into the wood shavings that covered the floor. She landed hard, and for a moment, she was stunned.

Twenty-two

"DON'T BOTHER screaming. No one will hear you. No one comes near this place since Edgar died." He was already pulling the door shut behind him.

"Wait!" she protested. But she heard the click of a padlock, and he was gone.

For a second, Aubrey wanted to cry. Tears started to well up, but she fought them back. Crying would solve nothing, she thought. She looked around her dim surroundings. She did know it. It was the same workshop that Taj had brought her to on their walk. The workshop where Maeve's father did his taxidermy. But Hadaway must be correct. Now that she looked closely, the place looked as if it had been abandoned in the middle of several projects. A thick coating of dust covered almost every surface. The only windows were small and high up around tops of the walls near the ceiling. She sat where she was, thinking.

What had she done that would land her in this predicament? She was in his house snooping around uninvited. He should have thrown her out. Maybe complained to Claire. But his reaction had been too intense. He had seen her near that particular ledger – she had been running her finger down the page. Maybe he even realized what she had been reading. *Something must be done.* And then his own admission – that he loved the place and didn't want to let it go. But Claire's *permission*? For what did he need Claire's permission?

She slapped her hand down on the wood shavings in frustration and surveyed her surroundings again.

How long would it take for someone to realize she was missing? What story would Hadaway tell at the dinner table? Worst case scenario: That her family had finally come for her. That she left without saying goodbye and thank you to her hosts?

How long could she last here?

Her mind got stuck. There was absolutely nothing in it, except for the dismal thoughts she fought to block as soon as they popped up. She absently played with the wood shavings on the floor around her. When she looked up a few minutes later, Maeve was drifting near the main work table. Maeve drew her hand along the table surface as she moved and then stopped to pet a beaver that was being crafted into a woodland scene.

"How are things going?" Maeve asked without looking up from the beaver.

Aubrey sighed, exasperated. "You tell me!" She gestured helplessly around her.

Maeve stopped and looked at Aubrey. "How are you going to find out how I died if you're stuck in here?" she asked accusingly.

"Your privilege is showing," Aubrey said under her breath.

"I heard that," Maeve cut back quickly. "You say that like privilege is a bad thing."

"Oh, I just mean get out of yourself for a while," Aubrey said in frustration. "Look at me, Maeve! No one would talk to me because I'm the outsider. I tried to get information the other way, and now I'm locked in here. No one knows I'm here. Your mother was contacting my supposed parents to collect me – you act like you're the only one with a problem!"

"I'm dead!"

For a moment – just a moment – Maeve's face turned horrible. There was a ferocity in her visage, and her eyes lost their remaining humanness. It was just for a moment, but it frightened Aubrey, and she gasped. Then Maeve was Maeve again. Her vaguely transparent self.

"I just don't know how much more I can do here if people won't talk to me," Aubrey said. "It's not like I can go back and see what happened."

Maeve's eyes shifted with thought. Her brows furrowed. She looked back at Aubrey. "Maybe you can."

"What?"

"Take my hands," Maeve directed.

"What? No!"

"I said, take my hands." She sounded like Claire, as she grabbed Aubrey's hands in hers. For cold, ghostly hands they felt oddly sharp.

"I said, no!" Aubrey tried to pull away, but the world shifted. Her lungs grew tight.

"HOW IS AUBREY DOING, Mrs. Harrison?" Gerard asked, handing her a hospital coffee in a brown paper cup. She looked small sitting in one of the dingy, light-aqua pleather chairs that lined the small waiting room outside the ICU. She glanced again at the clock, willing away the minutes before the next session of visiting hours.

"Thank you, Gerard. That was kind of you." She absently took a sip from the small opening in the plastic lid. She flinched as it scalded her tongue. At least she could still feel something. She took the cover off to let it cool.

"The doctors came in. They shined lights in her eyes, checked her reflexes. They say she isn't responding to anything. But I talk to her and hold her hand, and I swear a couple times she squeezed my hand. They say it was an involuntary reflex." She set the coffee on the small, magazine-covered table between the chairs.

"They make me so angry," she said, the frustration edging toward nastiness. "How do they know what she can hear? What she can do? I know what I felt!" She paused, closing her eyes. "And she responded to me," she added flatly.

"I bet she did," Gerard said. He sat in the chair on the other side of the coffee cup. She looked so lonely, like she needed company, any company.

She looked at him. "I'm praying like crazy, and I don't even know who I'm praying to."

He didn't know what to say. This was awkward, but he liked Aubrey. Really liked Aubrey. And he felt really badly about the accident. He bit the inside of his cheek nervously. He was poor company.

"I'm sorry," she said snappishly. "Look, it was really nice of you to come by, but there's no change. In fact, the doctors seem really worried. The longer she stays like this, the worse her chance of coming back to us. It's like she's running out of energy."

She closed her eyes again. "She just can't run out of energy."

Twenty-three

TRANSPARENT, Aubrey floated about three feet above the ground. It would have been a beautiful feeling if she hadn't been so panicked.

"Maeve! What have you done?"

Maeve, now flesh and blood, only blinked, having forgotten why she was there. She looked absently around her.

Her appearance interrupted the work of a man standing behind the large table. "Why, hello Maeve. I didn't hear you come in." Although the elderly man wore a leather apron and his shirt sleeves were folded up to his elbows, he bore the stature of a scientist rather than a laborer. He returned to his work, and with gloved hands began attaching a mounted serval to a rock.

Maeve stepped up to the work surface, but Aubrey flew in front of her. "Maeve! Look at me! Maeve!" But Maeve acted as though she didn't hear her.

Only it wasn't acting.

"Why, I've forgotten why I came in here!" Maeve said with feigned brightness. She stroked the serval under its chin. "Mother says I'd forget my head if it wasn't screwed on tight!"

The elderly man chuckled, but stooped closer to the delicate work.

"Hmmm," Maeve continued thinking out loud. "Maybe I was just missing Father. Yes," she said more confidently. "Yes. I was out walking, and I was probably just missing him."

The man looked up from his work and smiled fondly at her.

"No, Maeve! No! That's not what you were doing!" Aubrey flew between Maeve and the elderly man. "You were talking to me! And now –"

"This is really quite beautiful Mr. Brighton," Maeve said, unhearing.

"Thank you, Maeve. It was one your father had started. I thought, having some free time, I might finish it." He stepped away and opened a cabinet.

Aubrey hovered, watching the discussion. Where had this man come from?

"That's good of you," Maeve said to the man. She stroked the creature's back, as if it were a house cat.

Mr. Brighton turned back to place a wooden box filled with moss on the work table. He noticed her touching the animal and almost reprimanded her, but thought better of it.

"You know…" he started delicately. "I've finished

Bertie."

Maeve looked up quickly. She immediately smiled, but her eyes moistened at the same time.

"Bertie? Can I see him?"

"Are you sure?" Mr. Brighton said softly.

Maeve breathed deeply. "Yes. Yes, I think so."

Mr. Brighton turned from her and opened the doors of a large closet. When he turned back, he held a wooden base on which a magnificent white peacock was perched. The elderly man placed the bird near the edge of the work table, its long tail flowing nearly to the floor.

"Oh, Bertie," Maeve whispered. Mr. Brighton stepped away as Maeve approached her pet. She stroked its neck and chest. "He's as beautiful as ever, Mr. Brighton." She turned to him. "Thank you. Thank you so much."

"You're welcome, Maeve. I'll bring him up to the house when I'm done here, and we can find a suitable place for him."

Maeve hugged the elderly man fondly. "That would be wonderful. I'll go now and see if Mother has time to help me decide where he should sit."

She stepped toward the door, but turned back.

"I wish Father had taught me more about taxidermy. It is so truly fascinating. Perhaps I can persuade you to teach me as you were teaching him?"

"Perhaps," he eluded.

"Oh, Mr. Brighton…" Maeve teased. "We both know Mother will have a fit, but then again, she always does!" A self-satisfied smile played at her lips.

"I'll convince her. She won't blame you!"

Aubrey watched Maeve move back toward the door that only minutes ago Mr. Hadaway had padlocked shut. Maeve turned the handle and swung it open with no problem. Aubrey brought her hands to her face and pushed them into her hair as the situation finally began to dawn on her. Had time turned back?

Aubrey glided after Maeve. "Oh, Maeve! What have you done to me? Now no one can see *me*, but they can see *you*!"

Maeve started down the drive and veered down the pathway between the Old Fashioned Garden and the spot where the men were constructing the Rock Garden. As Aubrey glided behind, she knew it was as close to the work site as Maeve dared to go unaccompanied.

"Where *are* you going?" she asked as she stuck close to an unhearing Maeve.

The construction site was a flurry of activity. About a dozen men, aided by several teams of horses, pulled stones, dug and strained to rearrange nature to Mr. Hadaway's better judgement. The landscaper glanced in the girls' direction. At first, Aubrey was stunned by Mr. Hadaway's nonchalant demeanor. He had just caught her snooping around his cottage and locked her in the taxidermy shed. But instead of being infuriated at the sight of her, he hollered instructions in one direction and pointed in another. Then Aubrey realized that he didn't notice her because she didn't exist! Although only minutes had passed in her reality, somehow she had been shoved back in time. On *this* day, in *this* place, he hadn't met her yet. Aubrey closed her eyes in disbelief. How could this be happening? She glided silently behind Maeve, a nausea growing in her gut.

Although Maeve knew she shouldn't, she slowed her pace, so that she could take in as many details as possible. Aubrey knew Maeve found the work fascinating. It was as if she could read her mind, feel her emotions.

The workers had dug a small canyon and lined it with rocks. It followed a subterranean path and disappeared from view. A few men were planting a dogwood tree and hostas amid another grouping of rocks. Among stone crevasses, a smaller team of workers was planting more delicate plants – dog tooth violets? Maeve was dying to get a closer look. But no matter how slow her saunter, she was running out of pathway. She turned her steps toward home.

Aubrey watched Maeve walk in the direction of the house, but looking over her shoulder toward the workers, she noticed something interesting. Perhaps Maeve's stroll had given Aubrey the tip she needed to get started.

The coolness of the morning was slipping away. Warren stopped fighting the clay and rock to wipe his brow with his sleeve. He saw Maeve's slender frame in the distance as she strolled down the shaded path. He felt she was spying on them, not in a malicious way – just curious about this new garden. It was different from all the rest, more rugged, more natural. The lace dresses she wore would contrast with the rough-hewn stone and the lush greens of the woodland plants.

That was when he saw the handkerchief fall as she walked away. Unthinking – no, thinking only of her – he dropped the spade and rushed after her.

"Miss! Miss!" he hollered. Aubrey took note as the workmen stopped, cast knowing grins at each other, and chuckled.

Warren picked up the handkerchief from the ground as Maeve turned in her tracks. Aubrey watched as Maeve retraced her steps to where he was standing.

When Maeve was close enough, she reached out her hand to take back her handkerchief.

"Thank you," she said. For someone so delicate, her gaze was steely. Warren seemed suddenly aware of the dirt ground into his fingers, his rough work clothes, his stained cotton shirt, and soiled canvas pants. She was the most beautiful girl he had ever seen, lean and graceful. Her features delicate. And he was fascinated by her hair. Her flaxen hair – almost white – was braided and woven into a crown, then plaited into a thick braid that she let hang forward of her shoulder. He realized he was staring and averted his eyes. Maeve was sorry he looked away. He had unusual hazel eyes.

"I know it seems just a handkerchief, but my father gave it to me." She didn't need to explain. They both understood it was a reason to stand there longer when they both knew they shouldn't be.

"Gallagher!"

Warren jumped out of his stupor when he heard his boss's voice.

"Good day," he managed, touching his cap and giving a slight bow before running away.

Maeve heard the workers break out into raucous laughter as Warren returned to them. Before she turned away, she saw several workers doubled over, gripping their spade handles to hold themselves upright.

"Got yourself an audience with the princess!" one managed.

"There's in over your head!" laughed another.

"Settin' your sights a little high," said the mustachioed man closest to Warren. He slapped Warren hard on the shoulder, catching him off balance.

An older man in grey work pants and a soiled white shirt watched silently. The man noticed Warren redden, then, turned away as he noticed Mr. Hadaway, who disciplined Warren with nothing but a furrowed brow. It was enough.

Twenty-four

"DALTON." Claire Somerton stood at her desk, her hands flat on its surface, her head bowed in defeat.

"I don't know what I am going to do."

"Do?" Dalton was sitting on the settee in her office, his ever-present bowler hat on the cocktail table next to his tea saucer, the bone china tea cup paused before his lips. He set the tea cup back on the saucer, tea unsipped. "Do? You'll do as you've always done, dear. You'll be The Lady of Fairview."

"But Edgar was always so meticulous about the running of the estate. I can't even pretend to know all that he did."

"The place practically runs itself." Slight irritation dripped into his voice as he leaned forward and managed a sip of the tea.

"Do the men seem to be getting edgy?" She turned to him, leaning her thin frame against the desk. His irritation didn't go unnoticed by her. She crossed her arms over her chest.

"Edgy?"

"Do you always need to repeat the last word of my utterances? Yes, edgy. When I walk to the worksites, I catch sideways glances – and not pleasant ones, Dalton. Mr. Hadaway – although pleased with the payments coming his way for the development of the grounds – well, I can't help but catch tones that creep into his voice, condescending tones. I know I'm a woman – but I'm in charge now. I *will* be listened to." Her fist hit the top of the desk for emphasis.

"You're imagining it, Claire." He leaned back, crossing his leg on his knee. "Your fairer intuitions are overwhelming you."

She rolled her eyes. "Stop that," she ordered. With a toss of her head, she stepped to the window. A warm summer breeze stirred the lace curtain.

He chuckled. "Sorry to get under your skin, dear. But there *are* differences between men and women. We men go about things differently – business-like. You women see things with your heart. You go at things emotionally. Why even this. Edgar would have brushed it off. Just given the commands."

"Edgar would never have been treated like this to begin with."

"Hmm." Dalton leaned forward and sipped his tea, clinking the empty cup into its saucer. "You miss him, dear." She hung her head, silent. "We both miss him."

Maeve, perched in a wicker chair on the veranda outside her mother's office, sat as still as the statue of Diana the Huntress in the Blue and White Garden. She hadn't intended to eavesdrop. She had found her way back to Fairview, and as she often did, found a quiet corner of the home and was reading. It was such a beautiful day, the fresh air felt almost magical. In fact, the warm air mixed with the shade of the porch made it difficult to concentrate on the story, as another drama unfolded from the window next to her. Her mother, the always-in-control, perfection-expecting woman that she knew was in her office right now spilling her self-doubt out to Mr. Kendall. He had been her father's best friend. He still frequented the estate acting as her mother's confidant and – sometimes he seemed more than that.

She could not let her mother – or anyone else – know she had overheard the conversation. Little did Maeve know that someone else had overheard the conversation, as well – someone who was floating very near her wicker chair.

Twenty-five

HER MOTHER missed Father, too. There was some comfort in that.

Maeve quietly got up and moved across the veranda toward a door further away from her mother's study. Her parents had designed the house so that every room opened up to the great verandas that wrapped the house. She entered the library across the hall from her mother's study, and Aubrey floated in behind her. Maeve placed the book she had been reading on a table there. For a moment, she paused. Her hand automatically ran down the feathered back of a stuffed pheasant displayed on the table. Cautiously, she crossed the hall and hesitated at the door to the study with Aubrey close behind. Her mother was moving a vase on the mantle.

"Hello, Mother. Hello, Mr. Kendall." Maeve knew she was interrupting their meeting, but she had to see the all too infrequent grief on her mother's usually stoic face to make sure it was real. Claire sniffed and patted her hair into place before turning to greet her daughter.

"Maeve. You look lovely today. What have you been doing?"

"Well, I went for a walk," Maeve began. For a moment, she considered how much she should tell her mother.

"It's been a beautiful day for that."

"The funniest thing happened," Maeve ventured, watching her mother's expression carefully. "I ended up in Father's workshop, but I don't have any idea how I got there."

I could help you with that, Aubrey thought as she drifted up toward the ceiling to get a better view of everyone's face.

Dalton Kendall raised his eyebrows as he leaned forward to pick up his tea cup.

"That *is* unusual," her mother said. "But you know, Maeve, Mr. Kendall and I were just talking about your father and how much we both miss him. Grief stirs differently in all of us. Maybe you were just daydreaming as you walked."

"Yes, that's what I thought," Maeve said. "But something positive did come out of it."

"Oh?" her mother inquired.

"Mr. Brighton has...finished with Bertie."

A concerned glance sparked between Dalton and Claire.

"That's wonderful," Dalton murmured.

"Yes. Yes, it is," Maeve encouraged. "He wanted me

to talk with you, Mother, about a suitable place to display him. I would like it to be somewhere prominent, somewhere special."

"Well, do you have any suggestions?" Her tone was level, cautious.

"Perhaps in the salon?" Maeve suggested. "A table there? You can see into that room from the dining room, and I pass by it often during the day."

"I think that's a wonderful suggestion, Maeve," Claire said. "I'll tell Lindsay to make room for him."

"He's bringing Bertie up to the house as soon as he's finished working in the shop," Maeve added.

"I'll make sure I talk with her immediately then," Claire said, stepping over to her desk and picking up a small brass bell. "Before I ring for her, though, I wanted to tell you that Aunt Gladys and Magdalena and Lucas are stopping by tomorrow on their way to Albany – "

"Oh! Lena and Lucas? How wonderful! We haven't seen them in ages," Maeve cut in.

Her mother sighed, a combination of frustration at Maeve's bad manners and her enthusiasm at seeing her cousins.

"I'm sorry, Mother," Maeve said, realizing her rudeness.

"Yes, well. I'm pleased you're glad they're visiting. I was hoping you would be. I'll need you to entertain them a bit, while I visit with my sister."

"Of course!"

"I'm not sure if they will need to stay overnight. I suppose it depends when they arrive. I'll have Lindsay prepare for that possibility as well." With things now in order, Claire rang the small brass bell.

Twenty-six

"MAEVE!"

There was a clatter of silverware on china and chairs scraping the floor as two young children screeched, fled the breakfast table, and ran to embrace their cousin. Maeve squatted down to greet them and was nearly bowled over. They threw their arms around her neck. The older of the pair, a girl with brown wavy hair, tucked herself in Maeve's lap and, as a result, her brother tumbled to the floor. The girl, who was eight, stroked Maeve's flaxen braid, lovingly.

"We missed you so, Maevy," she said.

"I missed you, too, Lena. And you as well, Lucas," Maeve said, leaning over and drawing him back in. The little boy, who was two years younger than his sister, patted Maeve on the back and stood nearby. "Up now, Lena! You're growing so much!"

Maeve rose when the little girl stood up. She tousled

their hair, and the children followed her back to their seats at the table. Aubrey, who had been drifting in the doorway, followed them to the table and sat in one of the unoccupied seats.

"Aunt Glady, it's so good to see you." Maeve leaned down and gave her aunt a kiss on the cheek. "You must have travelled all night to arrive so early," Maeve said as she took her place at the table. A servant filled her plate with eggs benedict and then poured her tea while she addressed her aunt.

"It's not really all that early," she said with a smile. "I thought we could get a four or five hour visit and then be on our way again. Papa is expecting us in Albany in two days," she said, referring to her father, Maeve's grandfather.

"Anything wrong?" Claire asked from her end of the table.

"Oh, no, just a visit," Gladys said after she swallowed. "We haven't seen him in such a long time. James has been busy with business dealings, and the children and I just wanted to go visiting. We haven't seen you in ages as well, so this is a bonus!"

"You and the children can stay as long as you like, you know that," Claire said with a smile that Aubrey noticed was easier than with her own daughter.

"Thank you Claire."

"Your rooms are always waiting for you –"

"Papa's waiting for us…." Gladys sounded as though the temptation of the invitation was almost too much. "Perhaps on the way back through?"

"Oh, that would be delightful! We could really catch up then."

Aubrey noticed the children's eyes sparkle as they glanced at each other. Lucas could barely contain himself and began bouncing in his seat, but still kept quiet as both of the children had during the meal. Aubrey had to chuckle to herself at his excitement. Gladys smiled, too.

"Children, it seems you have finished with your breakfast," their mother said. "You can be excused if you are indeed finished eating."

"Thank you, mother," Lena said as she placed her napkin delicately next to her plate. Lucas wiped his mouth with his napkin and tossed it on the table not noticing his mother's scornful brows. The little boy jumped out of his chair and made to run from the table.

"Lucas." his sister said softly.

"Oh! Sorry, Momma. Sorry, Auntie Claire," he said, and returned to the table to push his chair back into place.

Claire touched Gladys's hand gently, and the two sisters smiled at one another. Aubrey looked from them to Maeve and recognized a comforted smile settle to her lips as well. Maeve realized she had not felt this much warmth at Fairview in quite a long time.

Twenty-seven

"I AM JUST FINISHING, too," Maeve said, leaving her breakfast half eaten. "Might I be excused as well, Mother?"

"Of course, Maeve," Claire said, pleased that her daughter had remembered their conversation.

The children caught Maeve's eye as they skipped past the table, unable to contain their excitement. She followed them to the doorway, but Aubrey remained at the table noticing the sisters beaming at each other.

Maeve paused just outside the door with the children, allowing the sisters to overhear the conversation.

"Lucas, Lena, what shall we do to entertain ourselves? Would you like to go bowling?"

Lena clasped her hands as though her prayers had been answered, but Lucas's eyes widened with the possibilities of an afternoon at Fairview. He motioned for Maeve to come down so that he could whisper to her.

"The last time we were here, we played zoo." He pulled away to see Maeve's face, and she smiled, remembering. "Do you think we could play that again?"

"Oh, yes!" Lena said. "Oh, Lucas, I had forgotten what a good time that was!"

"All right then," Maeve said. "Come help me find Father's pith helmet in the library and we'll look for some other props to add to our game." She took their hands in each of hers. As they walked past the archway that led to the dining room, Maeve made sure she saw the look of approval in both her and their mothers' countenances.

Aubrey was torn. She was still distraught about her current state of being, but tried to push those feelings down in order to tend to her mission. If she had any chance of regaining her life – she had been alive hadn't she? – she needed to find out how and why Maeve died. But there was a more immediate problem. Did her fact-finding mission have a better chance if she stayed here and listened to the conversation between Claire and her sister Gladys, or if she followed Maeve and two obviously innocent children? The women were already giggling like school girls over the newest fashions. Aubrey could see no connection between hem lengths and murder plots, so she drifted off after Maeve and the children. They were entering the library when she caught up to them.

"Here's Father's pith helmet," Maeve said, standing on tip toe and plucking it from a shelf.

"What about this bag?" Lena said, pointing to a

canvas satchel hanging on a coat tree.

"Good find, Lena!" Maeve said as she placed the pith helmet on Lucas's head. "You could wear it over your shoulder this way." She placed the bag over the girl's head so that the strap was across her chest and the bag hung at her hip. "You look like it's filled with food for the animals." Lena smiled at the idea.

"You need something, too," Lucas said searching the cluttered shelves.

"I know! I'll use this notebook and fountain pen." Maeve said, picking up the items from the desk. "I can be a visiting zoologist taking notes on the eating habits and habitats of your zoo's animals."

The children squealed in delight, and the trio trooped back down the hallway to the room Aubrey had always thought of as the "castle room."

"Welcome to the Fairview Zoological Gardens, Miss Somerton," Lucas said in a mock baritone voice. "This is my helper Miss Dunbar."

"Pleased to meet you Miss Somerton," Lena said as she drew herself up taller and held out her hand. As she shook Maeve's hand, they all giggled. "Let us show her around, Lucas."

"Yes, let's," he said. "Why will you be taking notes, Miss Somerton?"

"Ah, my notes," Maeve said. She put a finger to her chin and stared at the ceiling in thought. "For my studies, I need to know what types of animals you keep here at the zoological gardens and how much they eat. If you could kindly tell me that information as we tour, that would be wonderful!"

The children giggled again. Lucas adjusted the pith helmet that kept falling down over his eyes and took the lead.

"This is our bear," Lucas said, gesturing to the nearest piece of taxidermy, a bear posed trotting across an outcropping of rock.

"It can't just be a bear," Lena corrected. "It has to sound special. This is a zoological park, after all."

"Well? What would you call it then?" Lucas asked, hurt, his small hands on his hips.

"Uh…" Lena hesitated, caught in her lack of knowledge.

"I can see this is an American brown bear," Maeve cut in to solve the dilemma. "And he's quite tame!" She patted the bear on his head and tickled his ears. The children laughed, and Lena took some pretend food from her satchel and fed it to him.

"He eats oatmeal and eggs every day," she said.

"I don't think that's what bears eat," Lucas said, pulling his mouth into a pout.

"Ours does," Lena said. Maeve laughed. The game went on in the same fashion for some time. Aubrey noticed that Maeve laughed easily with the children. She was good with them – patient and kind. She was good at playing pretend and kept the game lively and fun. Aubrey also noted how often Maeve touched the animals. She stroked every one of them as if they were real, and Aubrey saw that when she did, her eyes became just a touch sad. She wondered if Maeve was feeling sorry for the animal or if the taxidermy made her miss her Father.

The game wove around the castle room and into the hallway where the trio paused for several minutes to discuss a collection of birds in a large glass case.

"What a beautiful habitat," Maeve said. "It looks so natural!"

"Yes," Lucas said. "The animals need a space that reminds them of home." He searched the cage for things to talk about. "They need branches to sit on and bushes to hide in. And you see the sky? They like bright skies – not a lot of clouds."

Maeve made pretend notes while he talked, her eyebrows raising now and then as if the information he gave her was groundbreaking. "Fascinating!" she said, and they all laughed.

Lucas looked for the next place to lead his tour. They were near the columned entrance to the salon, and he saw the new addition to the room. "Now the prize of our collection, Miss Somerton." He led them into the room to an oval table now featuring Bertie. "Our white peacock."

"Oh, he is beautiful!" Maeve said, walking up to him and gently stroking his neck and back. "Look at his wonderful tail." Ever so lightly, she ran her fingers over the feathers. So lightly, so as not to disturb them. A small pain shot through her abdomen. She was feeling Bertie's loss through to her core, she thought as a tear escaped her eye.

"He eats corn and oatmeal," Lena said, again pulling

imaginary food from her satchel and holding her palm up to his beak. "Why are you crying, Maeve?" she said, breaking character.

"He was my peacock. My Bertie. I thought I was ready to see him this way – I'll be all right. I'll get used to him." She stroked his back again.

"He was yours? A pet you mean?" Lena asked.

"Yes, sort of."

"And now he's like *this*?" Lena wrinkled up her face in disgust.

"Lena! That's not polite!" Lucas scolded.

"It's all right, Lucas. It is kind of strange, I guess. But I loved him, and I'd rather have him this way than not at all," Maeve said.

Lena pulled the satchel strap over her head and thrust it back at Maeve. "Can we go bowling now?" she asked.

Twenty-eight

MAEVE'S AUNT and cousins left after dinner, and suddenly the house was quiet.

Aubrey was starting to understand why Maeve liked the company so much. Fairview was wonderful and peaceful, but company brought it to life.

Aubrey found herself floating around the estate late the next morning, when she spotted Warren in the distance putting a blanket and saddle on Daisy, a chestnut roan. She was sure he was taking advantage of Mr. Hadaway's new rule. She had heard Claire discussing it with Dalton. Mr. Hadaway had instructed supervisors to give the workers breaks during days of the heaviest labor. He didn't want any more accidents to mar the stories of his beautiful gardens. Aubrey drifted closer. Warren added her bridle and rein. "It's okay girl," he said. "We're just going to get some exercise. We need that, you and me. Can't stand to be in just one small place, can we?" He stroked the horse's nose and patted her firmly on the neck before swinging into the saddle.

He rode her easy, walking the paths between the gardens with a transparent Aubrey trailing behind. Along the main drive, he ventured a trot, but nothing more, and only on the established paths. He didn't want to be reprimanded for tearing up the lawns. But if it had been just up to him, Daisy could have easily been brought to a gallop through the expansive Deer Park.

He was rounding a curve near the Japanese Garden, when they both saw Maeve walking up ahead. Aubrey noticed Maeve glance over her shoulder at the sound of the hooves, but she ignored the rider and kept walking. For some reason, it looked as though her action shook Warren's confidence. He slowed Daisy to a walk, measuring the distance, leisurely catching up.

Although Maeve walked with confidence, Aubrey noticed the slightest change in her gate. Maeve, too, was shaken. If she had to guess, Maeve was smitten. But Aubrey had learned something about the social mores of the day. Warren was a worker. She was sure Maeve realized this. Maeve was a member of a different societal rank. She shouldn't be alone with any boy, let alone one of the workers. Aubrey drifted closer to Maeve, and the closer she got, the easier it was to read her thoughts.

Yes, he was a worker, but if Fairview was going to be hers one day, Maeve needed to know how to handle the workers. Aubrey saw Maeve hold her head a bit higher, and pull her braid to the front of her shoulder. Aubrey was sure Maeve was deciding she should speak first, as was fitting the owner of the estate in charge of the workers. Aubrey saw Maeve shift her eyes briefly to the ground as the horse's front hooves moved alongside her. She looked up to the rider.

"Exercising the horses today?" Maeve said using what Aubrey knew was her best air of superiority.

"Yes, miss," Warren said. "At least this one. We both needed it."

The horse tried to look at Maeve, but Warren pulled the horse's head aside so it wouldn't breathe or slobber on her.

"It's a beautiful day." He tried to coax the conversation.

"Yes," she said, and Aubrey sensed a wall crumbling. Warren glanced at the sketchbook Maeve carried. He dismounted the horse, still holding the reins, and the horse followed obediently. Aubrey saw his mind racing. He eyed the small canvas bundle in her hand.

"Are you looking for a sketching place?" he asked.

Maeve eyed him suspiciously without turning her head. "Why, yes," she said. "There's a door in the wall behind the Hidden Garden that I find to be...well, charming. If it were smaller, it could be a fairy door, or a magic door to another world."

Her voice had taken on a dreamy tone.

"May I come along?"

"I suppose so," she said.

The three of them walked along until they came across the hedge that secreted the Hidden Garden. There, in the north wall of the estate, in the shadows of the hedge, was a small arched green door with massive hand-wrought hinges. Aubrey could see the door's aesthetic appeal – the way it was set into the stone wall, the tan and grey of the stones against the deep green of the door. She knew an artist's eye would appreciate the black of the iron hinges, with just a hint of rust here and there, and the shadows cast from an overhanging tree branch. It was a magical image, if one had a sense of imagination.

Warren looped Daisy's reins over a nearby tree limb, while Maeve immediately settled herself on the grass, her white lace dress spilling around her. Warren lingered near the horse, petting her neck.

Maeve opened the book she had been carrying, and even from where he stood, Warren could see it was a sketchbook. Tossing her braid behind her shoulder, Maeve unrolled the canvas pack to reveal an array of pencils, chose one and started to draw. She shifted her gaze from paper to subject as her efforts formed the shapes before her. Once the general scene was sketched, she started choosing colored pencils and blending tones to recreate the scene.

She looked up and winced. There was that vague ache in her stomach again.

"What?" Warren said, walking closer. "I think it is quite good."

"The colors just aren't as vivid," she said, excusing the small pain. "It's always a disappointment that it is such a pastel version of reality." She laid the sketch pad in the grass in frustration. "What do you do? Here, I mean. At Fairview."

"Anything Hadaway tells me to do." He stepped over to the hedge, his back to her. He plucked off a miniature leaf. Aubrey drifted closer to Warren, and as she did, she noticed her newly found radar was focusing in on him. The closer she got, the clearer were his thoughts.

"Ah, yes. You build the gardens." Maeve said. The handkerchief still hung in the air between them in her memory, but she couldn't let him know how important that moment had been for her.

Warren turned to look at her. Her tone of voice surprised him. Surely, she remembered meeting him before. He pushed back his cap and stepped closer to where she sat on the ground. He folded himself down beside her in the grass. He sat easily on his side, propped on one arm, legs extended. He was not unaware that Maeve was taking him in.

There was a sureness about him, and although he was not what one would have called tall, he was not short either. He wore dark green work pants and heavy soled boots that bore the remnants of dried mud. His white shirt sleeves were cuffed up a couple times, just enough to show his forearms, and Maeve noticed their strength. Light blonde hair stood out against his tan skin. His hands, too, knew work. The creases in his knuckles and his fingernails were outlined with the day's dirt.

Warren felt her staring at his free hand as he turned the small leave over in his fingers. It was the first time he looked at his fingers with a different eye. The cream lace of her dress was only inches away. Its delicacy. Its fineness. His eyebrows creased in thought. She would never know the toil that was his life.

Noticing his drawn brows, she spoke softly. "They're beautiful, you know."

"Hm?"

"The gardens." Although she wasn't sure she didn't mean his hands. "I truly enjoy them." Color rose in her checks at the suggestion her mind implied.

His eyes shifted from his hands to her face. The cream of her skin. The light freckles that danced across her cheekbones. The mesmerizing blueness of her eyes. He felt his own eyes catching in her flaxen hair and following the braid down her back. He caught himself. This was the owner's daughter!

"It's getting late," he blurted. "They'll be looking for me."

He jumped up, freed Daisy's reins, and flung his leg over the horse, urging it on, barely in the saddle. Nearby, a worker in grey work pants and a soiled white shirt momentarily stopped trimming a rose bush. He glanced up at the sound of approaching hooves.

"Wait!" The word escaped Maeve as she pivoted to watch him ride out of sight. What had scared him off, she wondered? She picked up the small leaf he had dropped as he fled and looked back in the direction he had gone.

He would see her again. He didn't care what the other fellows thought or said. That night, he waded into the pond as the sky darkened. He'd stolen a brush from the horse stable, and he used it now to scrub his fingers and hands in the moonlight. He couldn't really see how good a job he was doing, but they had to be better than they were. They'd get dirty again – there was no denying that. But he had never thought to scrub them before…before seeing her in that lace dress.

Twenty-nine

THE TEAM of twenty horses strained against the heavy load. The boulder was inched into position. Slowly.

"More!" Hadaway hollered.

Aubrey jumped a little higher into the air when the driver cracked the whip above the horses' heads, and again they strained and snorted into the cool morning air, their hooves digging into the ground. She had taken to following Warren about as he worked, since it often entailed seeing Hadaway. She found that her voyeuristic state allowed her to gather knowledge that her solid state did not. Without having to focus on fitting into the conversation, Aubrey found she was much more able to narrow in on body language and facial expressions. She felt she could even read most people's thoughts.

"That'll do," Hadaway snapped. He walked around the boulder to the east and stepped back, looking at the larger picture. "Brinkworth! Have the men unload the smaller boulders in a ridge along there... and there," he said, pointing to the area. "Leave a six-foot opening for a path. Curve it along like this," he said mimicking an invisible path in the air with his hands. "Fill in behind the ridge to reach grade level with those trees. Remember, above all, it needs to look natural."

Brinkworth nodded his understanding. As supervisor, he had memorized the drawn plans, but Mr. Hadaway often changed them, so he couldn't depend on his memory as much as on other jobs. Frank Hadaway was a boss unlike any other he had ever had. To most men, they were planting gardens, moving land. To Frank Hadaway, the work seemed more like a painter's canvas. He smiled to himself, pleased at the comparison. Everything had to be perfect. That boulder, for instance. If it wasn't in the exact location that Hadaway was picturing, there'd be hell to pay. Reading his mind wasn't easy. And he changed his mind often. That boulder might be in the right place now, but when the path was placed, he might decide the boulder's location was off by an inch or two. Brinkworth mopped his brow with a rag that he then jammed into his pocket.

It was at that moment that he noticed one of the workers approach Hadaway and doff his cap. Brinkworth paused, ready to lambaste the young man, but Hadaway looked ready to deal with him. It was that Warren kid. The one who had stopped to return a handkerchief to the owner's daughter the other day. Now, stopping to talk with the boss? The kid didn't know his place. He'd get his. Brinkworth shook his head and went back to deliver instructions to a nearby crew.

"Mr. Hadaway, sir. My name is Warren, sir."

"Yes, Warren." Hadaway was perturbed. The workers knew better than to approach him, but he had seen this young man on the job and knew him to be a good worker. He also had seen him around enough to know he had eyes for Maeve Somerton. The boy was a fool, but the young could be useful, he had found. The boy had bright hazel eyes and a charming smile that Hadaway noticed he used to his advantage. But there was nothing wrong with that. It was not unlike himself, he noted. His charm had won him favor and had allowed him to work his way up to quickly become one of the best known landscape architects among the more advantaged households of the country.

"I know you have your plans, sir, and really it is none of my business...." Warren cast down his eyes in a feigned submission that was not lost on Hadaway.

"You are correct, it is not," Hadaway replied. He raised his eyebrows, though, knowing that like himself, this boy would not be dissuaded.

The young Warren flashed his smiling eyes. "Miss Maeve has been to this site and is fascinated with your ideas."

"Really?" Was the young man telling the truth, or was he just playing at Hadaway's ample vanity? He was building this garden with Maeve in mind, the final move he felt he needed to gain the girl's affections – and her mother's approval.

"Yes. She has quite an imagination and loves fairies, and, well, this is a very magical garden. I thought that if you could do something special for the girl here. A place that she could come to gather her thoughts, that she would like that."

"I see." Hadaway was still taken aback by this worker's brazenness. How did he know so much about the girl? But it was a good idea. He was right. Every other garden he had designed with resting spots. This one had them, too, but fairies? Hmm. The cogs of his brain had begun to turn.

Thirty

FRANK HADAWAY unrolled the paper like a tablecloth onto the library's center table. It revealed a carefully shaded drawing of a garden house made completely of stone. Claire Somerton stood, hands clasped behind her back, studying three views displayed on the paper. Aubrey hovered over her shoulder.

"This," he said pointing with his finger, "is the front." His finger traced over columns of roughly cut stacked stone. "It will be a lovely place to rest. It will be open on every side to catch summer breezes. Sills will be of stone and generously wide for seating or use as side tables. Eventually, it will be dressed with ivy, and, situated in the glen, it should be shaded and cool. Inside," he pointed to another drawing, "on the east side there will be a stone bench near this arched window."

Claire made an approving noise and glanced over her shoulder for Maeve, who was oozing boredom while running a finger along the spines of books on a shelf.

Aubrey rolled her eyes at Maeve's behavior.

Mr. Hadaway followed Claire's gaze for a moment, and sensing a losing battle with Maeve, added a boost of enthusiasm to his presentation. "And, now this is the really exciting part! There will be a stone staircase to the upper level. The handrail will be formed with the vining trunk of a wisteria. Quite unusual. And up top, all around will be a castle parapet. It will be a garden house fit for a fairy princess."

Maeve, who had finally found a book that suited her mood, wandered over to study the drawings along with her mother and the unseen Aubrey.

"It is for you, Maeve," he said, stepping back and gesturing graciously. He tried to catch her eyes in a meaningful way, but Aubrey noticed Maeve never raised her eyes to meet his. Instead, she took a step back and ran her hand across the stuffed pheasant on the table there.

Mrs. Somerton lifted an eyebrow in her daughter's direction. "How very special, don't you think dear?"

"Oh, yes, of course." Maeve's tone was not convincing. Her attitude was underwhelming. Not at all the effect Frank Hadaway had been looking for.

"It will be the perfect place for Miss Maeve to read on a hot summer's day." He continued his pitch.

"It is a lovely idea, Mr. Hadaway." Claire's tone tried to make apologies for her daughter's rudeness. "What made you think of it? A garden house wasn't in the original plans."

For an instant, Hadaway thought of taking credit, but

instead took the opportunity to tell the truth and test his theory. "Actually, one of the young men at the worksite thought of it. He had seen Miss Maeve about the grounds and thought she would appreciate a rest stop during her strolls."

In a flash of recognition, Maeve's eyes widened and her pulse jumped. One of the workers? It had to be Warren, she thought.

Hadaway noticed he had Maeve's attention now, but not in the way he had intended. His theory was correct. When young Warren had approached him about the garden house, he had a vague suspicion of inappropriateness, but now Maeve's reaction confirmed it. Hadaway thought he masked his own face quickly enough. Claire's steely-eyed glance at Maeve made Hadaway believe she had caught Maeve's excitement as well. If Claire suspected an inappropriate dalliance on Maeve's part, her mother's approval would definitely turn in his favor. All he needed was something to secure his true plans.

Meanwhile, Maeve's brain flew to concoct an inarguable excuse to escape this meeting. "If you'll excuse me Mother, I'm not feeling well." It was partly true. Her stomach was aching again.

"But Maeve –" Claire began her protest, but Maeve's sharp tone silenced her.

"I really need to lie down," Maeve said. "Good afternoon, Mr. Hadaway," and with book in hand, she fled the room. Aubrey made to follow her, but paused at the doorway just long enough to hear Claire's apology.

"I am sorry about Maeve's reaction to your plan, Mr. Hadaway. It was truly generous of you."

"Well, you know my motivation, Mrs. Somerton. I want your daughter to be happy."

"Yes."

"When she sees the garden house rise magically from the ferns like a fairy castle, I know Miss Maeve will fall in love."

Thirty-one

WARREN WAS among the men standing about, receiving instructions for the next stage of the project. He leaned heavily on a shovel, awaiting his turn. A few men were being called out to assemble for wall building when a rustling of leaves nearby caught his attention, and he smiled. Warren quietly raised the shovel and poked his friend Miles as subtly as possible.

A conversation of eyes followed. Miles drew his brows together, and Warren responded with a subtle head tilt and eyes that shifted towards the underbrush. Miles's gaze followed the tilt of Warren's head, and after studying the shrubbery for a moment, he noticed an edge of lace revealing itself among the leaves. He smiled and nodded to Warren, who casually leaned his shovel against a tree trunk. He separated himself from the men by a short distance and bent over feigning interest in a nearby plant. Miles sneezed loudly, doubling over with the effort. Almost all the men shot their attention in the direction of the explosion, burst into laughter, and

Warren was gone. Only one man, a worker in grey work pants and a soiled white shirt, saw Warren slip away.

Warren jogged past Maeve grabbing her hand and pulling her after him. Mischievous laughter spilled from her. "Shhh!" Warren turned back to her, smiling broadly at the beauty of the sound. Aubrey glided quickly alongside the pair.

They ran toward the stables panting and laughing. Once inside, Warren led a horse from its stall and bolted the door closed. He hooked cross ties to the horse's halter and went to the end of the barn for a saddle. As he buckled the girth, Maeve stepped back from the massive animal.

"What are you doing?" she asked.

"We are going for a ride," he stated simply as if talking to a child.

"Won't you get in trouble?"

"Won't *you* get in trouble?" He laughed and continued. "I won't be missed for a while, and Miles will cover for me. He'll say I was sick or something."

He mounted the horse and held a hand down to Maeve. With a glance around she took his hand, and he hoisted her up behind him. She wrapped her arms around his waist as he walked the horse from the stable and onto the main road of Fairview.

"We'll be seen," Maeve said, her face near his ear. "You'll get me in trouble."

"So *now* you're worried!" He laughed again.

"Where are we going?"

"I'm going to take you to a place that is truly

beautiful," Warren said over his shoulder.

Aubrey had trouble keeping up as the horse galloped on, down the main drive of Fairview and out the front gates, down Charlotte Street and Main Street before Warren urged it into a field and out of the village. Maeve grew hypnotized by the rhythmic gate of the horse and just held on tight as fields and trees flew past. After what seemed to be a long time, for her arms were growing weary, she thought she glimpsed blue through the trees. The sparkling teal was a different hue than the radiant morning sky. But it was just a glimpse. It was gone before she had a chance to think more about it.

But then it was there again. And gone.

"What's over there?" Maeve asked pointing to the west.

"That's what I'm bringing you to see."

Warren slowed the horse and guided it through the trees to the edge of a hill. Below them more trees speckled the land that dipped and met the water of a lake that rested peacefully between hillsides. The trees on the far side of the lake reflected in its surface with almost as much brilliance as the real trees.

"Oh, my!" It was only a whisper, but Warren heard the amazement in Maeve's voice.

He coaxed the horse down a path closer to the water. A grassy field, scattered with several willows, met the water's rocky edge.

He dismounted, then lifted Maeve down from the horse. Maeve stood, awestruck as Warren stepped away to tie the horse to a nearby sapling. Warren turned to walk back to where he had left Maeve, but she had already wandered down to the water's edge. She sat and removed her shoes. Aubrey sat a few inches above the ground against the trunk of a nearby willow. She pulled her knees to her chest. She couldn't help but envy Maeve and Warren.

"Turn away," she said as she flung her shoes aside. He did, and she rolled down her stockings and tucked them with her shoes. She approached the wet and mossy stones with caution, the quiet lapping of wind-driven waves mixing with a distant squawking of shore birds overhead. She pulled the hem of her skirt up and let the waves play against her toes. Warren smiled at her childlike glee.

"It's rather cold!" she hollered back to him, and he laughed in reply.

Warren pulled off his work boots and heavy wool socks and rolled up his pant legs. He trotted down to join her. But he didn't stop at the rocks. He waded right in, splashing noisily as he went.

"Hey!" Maeve's protests combined with a grin as the cool water soaked the lace she was trying to protect. Warren only laughed more freely. He stooped and scooped the water in a rowdy splash in Maeve's direction. It soaked her with some of the droplets even reaching her face and hair.

"Now that's not fair!" A mischievous glint shown in her eyes. She bent low, and letting go of her hem, used both hands to repeatedly scoop cascades of water in Warren's direction. Laughing, he took a step backward to avoid the onslaught, tripped and fell backward into the shallow water with a splash.

Maeve threw her hands into the air, victorious, and laughed until she could not breathe. Aubrey found she was laughing, too.

Cautiously, Maeve held out her hand to him. "Now, if I help you up, you won't pull me in, will you?" she asked. A glint sparkled in his eye, and he grinned. "It wouldn't be very gentlemanly of you."

"Who said I was a gentleman?" he joked, then sobered. "I won't." He took her hand, and she helped him up.

They walked up the shore, and Warren collapsed on the ground in the shade of a willow. He looked up at her and patted the ground beside him. "Rest a bit."

Aubrey leaned around the trunk of the tree to see Maeve sit on the grass and arrange her skirts around her.

"I've always thought Awagashat was an odd name for a lake." Maeve kept her eyes down as she fussed with her skirt.

"I like it," Warren said, decisively. "The Senecas named it. It means 'I might remember it.' And now I know I will."

She would remember this, too, she thought. "It's beautiful," she said turning her eyes to the rippling waters of the lake.

"Yes, it is," Warren replied.

Maeve turned expecting to see his profile gazing at the same lake view as she, but instead found his gaze still riveted on her. Aubrey turned back to stare at the water.

Hearing was enough. She could imagine the rest.

"I thought you brought me here to show me something beautiful," Maeve said.

"Ah!" Warren leaned back on his elbows, stretching out his legs and crossing his ankles. "Maybe I was being selfish. I know I wanted to look at something beautiful, and I am."

"Warren, stop." It was the first time she had used his name, and it sounded wonderful coming from those lips.

He pushed himself up and leaned into her. "Say my name again," he whispered. He was too close to her. Maeve felt her pulse race, and a warmth flooded her.

"Warren," she obeyed.

He brushed stray hairs back from her face. Maeve froze at his touch and realized she wasn't breathing. His fingers traced the line of her face, her jaw, and he cupped her chin in his hand. He drew in closer. Their lips met and the world stopped.

Thirty-two

SHE KNEW IT HAD been too long a kiss. She had melted into him. His hand had found the back of her head, and she had felt his fingers tangled in her braid. She had felt like she was drowning, never to breathe again. But when she pushed away, he let her.

Maeve's breath came quickly then. And so did her concern.

"Warren," she stammered. "Take me home. Please."

His face was still close to hers. She felt his breath. She closed her eyes as he brushed his lips against hers again. She opened her eyes to meet his. "Please."

Warren swallowed, and for a moment, gazed off toward the water lapping against the stones. Aubrey stood there, transparently staring at him. She understood too well the struggle in his heart. Quietly he stood and offered Maeve his hand. She stood and straightened her dress and hair as Warren retrieved the horse, who was munching grass nearby. He mounted the horse and helped Maeve up in front of him this time. He wrapped his arms around her as he took the reins. Maeve could feel the strength of his arms and shoulders. His closeness was disconcerting.

He brought the horse to a gallop at breakneck speed. Maeve felt herself panting for breath again. Aubrey flew behind them on their headwind.

"Please slow down, Warren!" Maeve hollered, but he either didn't hear her or didn't consider the option. Rather, he drove the horse on with a quick kick of his heels. Maeve closed her eyes and wrapped her hands in the horse's mane. Their pace didn't slow as they rode through the village or through the gates of Fairview. Warren only pulled up on the reins as they neared the stables. He rode around to the side of the building and helped her down off the horse rather roughly.

They said nothing as Warren rode the horse slowly into the stable without looking back.

It was then that Aubrey saw a man in grey work pants and a soiled white shirt slip behind a tractor. She didn't think he had been seen by either Warren or Maeve, both of whom had their minds on other things.

Aubrey could translate the bewilderment on Maeve's face as she followed her back toward Fairview. She could hear Maeve's confusion. What had she done to offend Warren? If anything, he had offended her. He had been bold to take advantage of her. But she had kissed him back…. Thank God no one had seen. She knew there was a difference in their social standings, but maybe there would be some way they could make things work out. No matter. He should have been apologetic, more genteel, she thought.

Maeve ran up the steps of the veranda and threw open the wooden screen door that led to the library. She flopped into a wicker rocking chair to contemplate the matter further, but failed to notice her mother putting a book back on a shelf behind the door.

"And where have you been Maeve? You look atrocious."

Maeve jumped up from the chair, and Aubrey spun in mid-air. "I took a walk," Maeve said, suddenly nervous about her appearance. She just now noticed the wetness of her dress. The sand and moss from the lake's edge still clung to the lace at the hem.

"A walk," her mother repeated, too calmly.

"Yes." Maeve hesitated searching for the best scenario. "Down by the Japanese Garden. I stepped onto the rocks at the edge of the pond to get a closer look at a tadpole I saw. Oh, Mother, he was wonderful! His legs had formed but he still had a fat tail! I lost my footing on the rocks and splashed in, I'm afraid." She cast her eyes down. She had never lied like this before. How easy it was.

Her mother walked over to a window. The sun shone through on an envelope she held. Claire tapped it lightly against her other palm, and she looked across the vast lawn toward the front gate. As Maeve followed her mother's gaze, she could see just a curve of the main drive between the trees. If the timing had been right, her mother could have seen Warren and her riding onto the property.

"It's a beautiful day to be by the water." Her mother let the statement hang in the air as she continued staring out the window.

Maeve wanted to tell someone how wonderful the day by the lake had been. She wanted a companion to discuss how confused she now felt about it all, but not her mother.

"Yes, it was quite relaxing," she lied again.

Thirty-three

"I'M GLAD YOU found it relaxing," her mother said. As she turned from the window, her face was cold and stoic. "Because I have some things that need to be tended to."

"Let me change, and then we can talk, Mother." Maeve's eyes still gleamed with her inner happiness.

"No." It was decisive, the way her mother got at times with the staff. She seemed to be standing taller. Aubrey raised her eyebrows at the turn the conversation was taking.

"All right." Maeve stemmed her enthusiasm and seated herself on the edge of the sofa.

"I have some business to discuss with you that needs your full attention. Someday Fairview will be yours." She turned from the window again, the envelope still in her hand. "I have found things challenging since your father died. He ran this estate flawlessly. Effortlessly. As the woman of the estate, I had my duties as well." She gazed off for a moment. "But now – now, I must fulfill both of our duties if Fairview is to remain solvent. When your father died, I did not know what to do."

"You spent time traveling," Maeve said absently.

"Yes. It was during those travels that I discovered a new focus."

"Improvements to your gardens," Maeve offered.

"Yes. I was so inspired by the gardens I saw while I was abroad that I brought back ideas, sketches – gardens and landscapes of which I thought your father would have approved."

"How come you are telling me this now?"

"I'm sorry, Maeve. We grieve in our own ways. I am ashamed to say that I was so distraught, I forgot that you needed me as well. I am sorry that I had nothing to give you." Claire's eyes were vacant. Maeve wasn't sure her mother was being sincere.

"It's all right mother." It was the right thing to say in view of things.

"No, it's not all right. Never say it's all right!" Claire slapped the envelope she was holding onto the table. She took a moment to gather herself. "Women say that too much. This estate – its legacy – that will be the only thing I will be able to give you that might make up for my shortcomings."

Maeve didn't know what to say.

"But I won't have you as ill prepared as I was. Obviously, you are already learning the duties you will have as the woman of the estate, but I want you to also be aware of the other duties."

"So that I will be able to do them? Like you?"

"My hope is that you won't have to. That is what I want to talk to you about. It's time."

Aubrey didn't like the sound of that, and she could tell by Maeve's instant frown that she didn't either.

"Time?"

"Maeve, you are seventeen. Most young ladies are betrothed by that age."

"Betrothed?"

"Yes. And Mr. Hadaway has asked for my permission to court you."

"Mr. Hadaway? Mother, he's old!" Maeve collapsed into the sofa, her emotions reeling, grasping for something solid to hold on to, but her mother pressed on.

"Not really, Maeve. He is twenty-eight and extremely accomplished and well respected for a man of so few years. He has a very promising future ahead of him."

"You're marrying me off?" Maeve stood in disbelief.

"Of course not. He would need to meet with your approval. I only ask that you spend time with him and give him a chance."

"But Mother, I don't love him!"

"Love him? Maeve dear, love is not instantaneous as it is with all your books. Love grows. Why, it's as easy to fall in love with a rich man as…" She turned back to the window, her tone changed. "…As with a poor man."

That was it. Maeve knew that her mother had seen.

"Why do you say that Mother? Why do you say it

like that?"

Holding up the envelope, Claire turned on her. "Because I just received this. Slid under a door to the house. One of the maids brought it to me. It is hand written. Roughly. Someone on the estate has seen you Maeve."

Aubrey knew instantly who it had been.

"I saw you as well," her mother said. "But *I* can keep a secret. Others cannot be trusted with such information. We will be scandalized."

Maeve stood and took the letter from her mother. Claire let her. Maeve flipped open the envelope and pulled out the note. Her eyes scanned the contents feverishly.

"I don't ask much of you Maeve. I never have, and maybe this is my fault, but you *will* do as I say now. *You will* allow Mr. Hadaway to court you."

"But –"

"And you *will* marry him."

Thirty-four

FRANK HADAWAY watched as Maeve burst through the wooden screen door onto the veranda and fled down the steps and across the lawn. He had been sitting in a wicker chair sipping iced tea, waiting for the moment when she accepted the courtship offer. Instead, she ran right past him without even seeing him.

But Aubrey, who had been gliding after her, stopped. She didn't like the look on his face. She glided closer and concentrated. Really concentrated. Then it started to become evident.

Although a confident man, Hadaway was not a stupid man. He was not so old that he had forgotten the power of first love. He knew now what he had to do. Surrender was inevitable. He knew he would have to lose a battle to win the war. Hadaway was not a stupid man.

He set down his iced tea glass on the small wicker table, rose, and made his way across the veranda and across the lawn with the confidence of a man in control of his destiny, if not the destinies of everyone around him.

Maeve would make a fine wife. She was young, beautiful, well-mannered, and well-read. But, if that arrangement didn't work out, he would make himself available to Claire. She was older than he, but not by much, and she was already cracking under the pressure of running the estate, something he was much more capable of doing. But that was the alternative plan. He would see if this first plan would come to fruition.

Aubrey glided in his wake as he strode to his cottage, changed into clothes more fitting for the field, and walked to the job site. He mulled over his options as he strode to the Rock Garden. There was some sense of urgency. He needed to reach that young worker, what was his name? Ah, yes, Warren. He needed to reach the young Warren before Maeve did. She would probably go off and cry by herself for a while before she tried to find him. Young girls were very predictable.

At the thought of Maeve, Aubrey began to lose focus. Like a radio that was plagued with interference, Aubrey was able to watch the scene, but could not hear.

As the worksite appeared over the knoll, Hadaway searched the sweaty faces of the workers for Warren. There he was, working on the foundation of the new addition to the site – the castle-like garden house that had been Warren's brainchild. It was too bad, he thought as he stood there surveying the operation. Warren was intelligent and hardworking. Hadaway could identify with the boy. Hadaway, too, had come from meager beginnings, but through hard work had accomplished so much and had come so far. With the proper guidance, Warren, too, could have gone places, Hadaway was sure. But that was not to be. No matter how it turned out, Warren would be at the losing end. Hadaway knew he had to make sure of that.

"Warren!" he called out from his post on the knoll. Warren looked up, his face streaked with dirt and sweat, as he tried to make up for his absence. He wiped his hands on his trousers and walked to where Hadaway was standing.

"Yes sir?"

"I wanted to thank you for your suggestion the other day. I see you are already making your vision become a reality."

Warren looked back at his work and then at Mr. Hadaway with a smile. "Yes, sir. I take it that the ladies of Fairview were pleased with the idea?"

"Why yes, of course, or we wouldn't be building it, now would we?"

"I suppose not," Warren said.

"And I made sure," Hadaway continued, "that the ladies knew the idea came from one of the workers. I knew the young Maeve would know who I meant." Here he gave Warren a conspiratorial wink which made the blood rush to Warren's cheeks.

"I don't know how you're going to pull it off, boy, but that girl's a catch. With some guidance, you might be able to make it happen. I am in need of an assistant, which, frankly, would raise your social status and would perhaps make such a union more plausible in the eyes of her mother."

The frank conversation was beginning to make Warren uncomfortable. Was this man – his boss, the famous landscape architect Frank Hadaway – making him an offer to be more than a worker so that he could have a life with Maeve? He hadn't realized that his feelings about her had been that obvious. He hadn't intended them to be. He thought they were being covert, not that the feelings weren't real. But somewhere inside he realized there could never be a future where his feelings for Maeve were concerned.

"While I work on arrangements at my end, and of course, put in a good word for you with Claire Somerton, you make sure you make strides with the younger lady of the house. As a man, I find small gestures are often the most appreciated. She'll be dining with her mother on the veranda this afternoon. I checked with the staff and quail on a bed of wilted watercress is on the menu. There are some delicious greens growing over along that ridge," here he raised his chin to indicate the direction – a motion so subtle none of the other men nearby would have noticed, although a few had noticed the now lengthening conversation between the young worker and the famous landscape architect.

"The plant should have some small white flowers on it this time of year. The leaves are fern-like. Those are what you want. But here –" he pulled some canvas gloves from his back pocket and handed them to Warren.

"Make sure you wear gloves. The leaves are very tender and delicate. If they touch human hands – they will wilt beyond use. Take them right to the kitchen, and have the girl who receives them wrap them in a towel, then give her the gloves so that she can prepare them properly. Mixed with the watercress, it will taste scrumptious. Maeve will notice the difference, and again, it will be all your idea."

Warren stared blankly at Mr. Hadaway.

"Go, now. This will be a wonderful surprise for her. It will be the most delicious dish she's ever eaten, and she'll have you to thank for it."

Warren's head was spinning with the suggestion, but thanked Hadaway and turned to gather the suggested leaves. Aubrey followed him, and as she turned to glance over her shoulder, she saw Hadaway smile slyly as he watched Warren walk away.

Thirty-five

SOME OF THE plants were almost as tall as he was, but Warren knew that the smallest of plants were always most tender. He pulled on the gloves and began to pluck the fern-like leaves from the stem of the plant. He was struck by the odd color of the stem, with its purple blotches on deep green. What *was* this plant? He had forgotten to ask Mr. Hadaway, who surely, as a plant expert, would have known.

It didn't matter, Warren thought. As long as it made Maeve's day better. How astute Mr. Hadaway was in realizing that was important to him. It was why he had taken Maeve to the lake earlier. He just wanted to show her something beautiful from his world. He paused in his work to remember – he sighed. It had been a wonderful morning, but then reality had crept in. Now maybe with Hadaway in his corner, the future might be different.

He gathered the last few leaves and walked them to the house. Surely, Hadaway hadn't intended him to stay away from the work site forever. He followed the drive around to the back kitchen entrance, Aubrey trailing after him. He rapped his knuckles on the wooden screen door.

A waif of a girl with tiny features and her hair tied up in a scarf appeared behind the screen. "Warren!" she exclaimed a little too loudly. She glanced over her shoulder in anticipation of being reprimanded. "I can't meet with you now!" she whispered.

Blood flooded Warren's cheeks for the second time that day. "Hello Meg," he managed. "It's not that. I need a favor."

Aubrey noticed that her small face looked crestfallen, but she put on her prettiest smile again quickly. "Of course, Warren. You know I'd do anything for you. What is it? I have to hurry. They're needing me for the dinner preparations."

"That's exactly what I need help with." He held up the greens to show her, and she opened the screen door to lean out to get a better look. "You're making wilted watercress today, aren't you?"

"Yes…" she hesitated, brows gathered at the sight of the greens he was displaying.

"These need to be mixed in. They'll make it tastier."

A loud commotion on the road made Aubrey lose her focus on their conversation. Men's voices hollering. Whips cracking. Horses whinnying. And a gruff man's voice shouting over it all. Aubrey drifted a bit toward the road to see what the fuss was about. Glancing over her shoulder, in the direction of the house, she saw the girl duck back into the kitchen. Her smile had disappeared.

"Pull!" A man's voice was a hollered blast. It was

accompanied by the clopping and scraping of hooves on macadam. Through the trees and around the bend came a team of horses pulling a flat-bed wagon which was carrying a massive carved stone dome. The man who was hollering stood in front of the dome on the wagon bed. Other workers, sweat pouring down their faces pushed at the back of the wagon or walked along side of the horses, holding their bridles and encouraging the animals with shouts.

"Hemlock." The word, spoken sharply at the kitchen door, caught Aubrey's attention. Wasn't that what had killed Socrates? Her attention snapped back to the house. She didn't know who said it, Warren or the girl from the kitchen. But she saw Warren turn, pound down the steps, and race toward the Rock Garden. He was moving so fast, she could have never caught up to him.

While Warren was at the kitchen door, Frank Hadaway was stealthily entering the front door. He was allowed entry to Fairview whenever he wanted and came and went at leisure, but this was one entry he wanted to keep under wraps if at all possible. He entered the massive main hall with its stone fireplace and abundant taxidermy. Instinctively he glanced at Maeve's bedroom balcony. The door was open, and she appeared not to be there. He paced quietly across to the corridor from which flowed the billiards room, dining room, living room and eventually the library and Claire's study. As he passed each room, he peered in, checking every possible dining spot. Since each of the rooms boasted a doorway that led to a balcony or veranda, the possibilities were numerous. He paused near the dining room, but no sounds came from The Bower. A door led outside between the living room and the library, but again, there was no clink of silverware on china. He cautiously entered the library with its many doors to the outside. The one straight ahead led to the veranda, which overlooked the Italian Garden. It was from that direction he thought he heard a chair move. And then sharp words.

"Maeve, Maeve! Are you all right?"

It was Claire's voice, and now she was yelling. Yelling for help.

He heard doors slamming against their frames elsewhere in the house and the pounding of feet on the wooden porches. He didn't need to know more. He slid back down the hall as quickly as possible. As he burst through the front doors, he paused only briefly as the afternoon sun hit him squarely. He mustn't run, he knew that. And so, he fled swiftly down the steps, just short of running, head held high, looking as though he had somewhere important to be.

But as he bounded down the steps, his shoulder rammed into something. It was the oddest feeling. Even though he knew nothing was there, it had truly felt like he had run into something or someone. It was a strange enough occurrence that he briefly looked over his shoulder to the spot in the middle of the short flight of steps where it happened. The glance reassured him that nothing was there. Even though his shoulder ached a bit, he couldn't stop to puzzle it out. He had to keep moving.

At the moment Frank Hadaway was fleeing down the front steps of Fairview, transfixed on a spot midway down the flight of stairs, an Aubrey who was becoming more alive by the second, appeared on the veranda at the other end of the house. Her shoulder throbbed and her head hurt, but her attention was drawn to Maeve, who lay unconscious near the table. There were several people about, some kneeling by her, others standing nearby wringing their hands or worrying a dishcloth. Aubrey went to her and quietly spoke her name.

"Maeve?" she said offering her hand. Maeve opened her eyes and looked at Aubrey, and raising herself on one elbow, unquestioningly took Aubrey's more solid hand. Aubrey walked a transparent Maeve a bit away from the scene. Maeve tried to look back over her shoulder.

"Don't look back Maeve," Aubrey said quietly. "It won't do any good."

Thirty-six

"HOW ARE you feeling Maeve?" Aubrey asked cautiously. Somewhere in her memory, she recalled that the pain of her accident had dissipated when Maeve helped her up.

"I'm fine," Maeve said. "I'm just worried about them." She looked back over her shoulder, but the veranda was empty.

"I told you not to look back Maeve."

"I've died again, haven't I?" Maeve looked sad.

"We couldn't have stopped it, Maeve. That's not why you brought me here," Aubrey reminded her. So many times, the mind needed prompting here, she noticed.

"That's right, I remember now," Maeve said, although her eyes didn't brightened the way Aubrey had expected them to. "You were to help me find out how I died. That was the moment, wasn't it?"

"Yes." Aubrey kept a watchful eye on Maeve as they

strolled slowly along the veranda. As difficult as Maeve could be at times, Aubrey felt her heart ache for this girl she had known only a short time. Maeve seated herself in a wicker rocking chair and smoothed her white lace dress across her lap. Aubrey knew the motion by now. It was the same one that Claire Somerton used when she knew difficult information was coming that she needed to steel herself for. Maeve was so like her mother, no wonder her mother had wanted so much for her.

"Well?" Maeve smiled ruefully. "I've had to live through that again. Actually, die through that again. It was not pleasant either time – although the feeling does fade," she murmured as she continued to fuss with the lace on her skirt. "Have you found out anything, Aubrey? Was I – murdered?"

Aubrey, who continued to stand, hesitated, debating how to begin. The news was damaging. Well, it would be damaging to a *living* girl. How would a spirit take it?

"This is going to be difficult to hear, Maeve," Aubrey dodged.

"I realize this, Aubrey, but it is why I brought you here. I expected you would tell me something I didn't want to hear. I don't *want* to be dead."

"Well," Aubrey began. "Just now, you appear to have taken ill during your meal with your mother. It was to be a mending time of sorts for you both. You had had a disagreement about a courtship with Frank Hadaway –"

"Ugh," Maeve interjected, quite uncharacteristically. "Don't remind me about that! I agreed to have the afternoon meal with her because she is my mother. I was never going to agree to the courtship. Not when I –"

"When you have feelings for Warren?"

Maeve looked up abruptly. "How did you know that?"

"Oh Maeve," Aubrey said with exasperation. "I've been watching you. We're both – well, we've got a lot in common."

"Yes." Maeve's eyes narrowed. She remembered something.... Aubrey and Warren. Near the Hidden Garden. Had there been a kiss? She couldn't remember. There were so many things her that frustrated her. She looked back down at her dress, smoothing it with growing ferocity.

"Maeve, I need you to understand. I don't have all the information yet. But I can tell you what I saw." Aubrey looked across the lawn, weighing her words.

"Yes, please do." Maeve's response was curt enough to shock Aubrey's full attention back to where Maeve sat on the porch.

"Just an hour or so ago, Warren was talking with Frank Hadaway near the Rock Garden," she began. "Warren seemed animated during the discussion. Then he walked to a field way over on the edge of the property where he picked some greens. He was wearing work gloves. I thought it odd at the time."

This time Maeve did look up, eyes widened with curiosity. "Go on," she said.

"He took the greens up to the house, to the kitchen door, and talked with one of the help – Meg, I think."

Maeve gave a disgusted huff at the girl's name. "I

don't understand. Why did he wear gloves? What did they talk about?"

"I didn't hear all of what they said, Maeve. A work crew came through with a team of horses. There was hollering and –"

"But why the gloves?" she interrupted.

"I'm really not sure," Aubrey said, her frustration growing. She took a breath. "I did see them talking for a moment. Warren asked her if she'd do him a favor, and then the crew came through. They were loud. Above all the commotion I heard one of them say the word 'hemlock.'"

"And he gave it to her to put in my dinner?" Maeve stood and began pacing.

"Maeve, we don't know that."

"She's made advances on Warren before, but he would never –" There was a gleam in Maeve's eyes that Aubrey had never seen before. Her hair, normally plaited neatly, began to stir from its tight braid as if fighting a small whirlwind.

"Calm down, Maeve," Aubrey said, suddenly frightened by the energy Maeve seemed to be emanating. "I really feel this has to be thought out. Something's missing."

Maeve had stopped her pacing, her hands balled into fists at her sides. Had she been a living girl, Aubrey would have thought she was going to strike her. She knew Maeve couldn't do that, but what *could* she do?

"Maeve!" Aubrey tried to stop what appeared to be a small tornado, the eye of which was Maeve. Her dress danced and whipped in a frenzied circle and then she began to fade from Aubrey's view. Quickly. But it wasn't the disappearance that alarmed Aubrey. It was the fire she saw in the specter's eyes.

"Maeve! No, No! Come back! We need to talk about this! Remember, he had been talking to Frank Hadaway!"

There was no response. Nothing visual. Nothing auditory. Aubrey even stood still for a moment and listened with her mind. Nothing. Aubrey began to panic. Where would Maeve go? What was she capable of doing? She had to find Warren. She didn't know why she thought that, but she knew enough of live girls her age – scorned girls, or girls who thought they were scorned – who went right to the source.

"OH SHEILA! HAL!" Lenora said, embracing each of them. "It was *so* good of you to come." There was a desperate sincerity to Lenora's voice. The women hugged again outside Aubrey's ICU cubicle, and Lenora buried her head on Sheila's shoulder. The women had been close until Lenora's husband, Wayne, up and left. He was Sheila's brother. Where Wayne had once been, only an awkwardness remained, both women feeling a responsibility for the man's actions.

"We came as soon as we heard, Lenora." The apology in Sheila's eyes spanned decades. "We couldn't let you bear this alone."

Lenora gently pushed herself away to arm's length and wiped an eye. She acknowledged the man and the girl of about twelve, who stood patiently waiting behind Sheila.

"It's good of you, really, but you travelled so far."

"Oh, not really," Sheila lied. About a year before, the Whitaker family had moved into an old inn, renovating it and opening it as a bed and breakfast. "Now, how is Aubrey?"

"I'd like to say she was doing better, but I don't think she is. There is no change. If anything, that makes it worse, although they tell me not to worry."

"How did it happen?"

"She was volunteering at the Fairview Estate. It was only her first day. They told me she fell backwards down the stairs outside the house. Landed on the sidewalk. Hit her head." Lenora's eyes started to fill with tears again. The young girl, Aubrey's cousin, covered her mouth with her hand, hiding a small gasp.

"Could I go in to see her, Aunt Lenora?" Lenora remembered the young girl, Samantha, as being much more reserved, shy even.

"Samantha, I'm sure Aubrey would like that. She was always fond of you. Don't let it scare you. Just hold her hand. Be careful to not bump any of the tubes. You can talk to her. They say it's good for her. And here, you have to put on a gown."

Lenora helped Samantha with the yellow paper gown, and Samantha slipped inside the glass room. She walked right up to Aubrey's bed and gently took her hand.

Thirty-seven

OH, ALICE, which, side of the looking glass are you on?

Aubrey gathered her skirts and ran as quickly as her tight shoes would carry her. She knew where she had to go.

No journey had ever seemed more dire. Her legs and feet seemed clumsy, unable to cooperate with each other, to coordinate toward their destination – which was where, exactly?

Aubrey had to find Warren, but where? She lurched to a stop, eyes, mind searching. Her mind told her the Rock Garden, but logic told her that was useless. The Rock Garden was finished. The workers wouldn't be there. But her body fled in that direction anyway. She ran through the rock canyon, under the rock bridge and out the other side and up the path. She turned left on the stone steps that led to the stone garden house, but found it difficult to find a fast pace on the uneven treads. At the top of the steps, logic confirmed no one was there. With agonized desperation she ran up the stone steps, her hand brushing the wisteria vine railing of the garden house. She mounted the crenellated roof. She paused. Heart thumping madly. Breathing heavily. Her hands resting on the cold, grey stones in front of her.

"Warren? Where are you?" she called weakly.

Somewhere beyond the chirp of crickets and gentle buzz of cicadas, men's distant hollering reached her. She listened acutely, focusing.

It was there – from over near the Secret Garden. She flew as fast as her feet could carry her. Back in the direction of Fairview. But behind it. Circumventing it. Maeve had too much of a head start and didn't need to depend on feet and wasn't bound by breathing. Who knew how fast she could travel?

Aubrey cut between the Rose Garden and the Italian Garden, down the pergola hung heavy with purple wisteria and yellow trumpet vines. She stopped at the end, listening tentatively. The men's voices seemed to be coming from a small copse of trees. They were louder now. She was almost there. But surely Maeve had been quicker.

Sprinting across the lawn, Aubrey entered the wooded area. The trees gave way to a clearing almost immediately. Set in the clearing's center was a large round platform of stone, obviously meant as a base for a building of some sort. She tried to take in the scene quickly, to locate Warren.

Yes! There he was!

He and at least a dozen other men, old and young, were pushing five stone Corinthian pillars into place around the edge of the circular platform. Four had already been set, and the men were working on the last. Although the columns appeared to be one piece, they were not. Several men set the base and then others hoisted chunks of the fluted column into place like building blocks one atop another, carefully lining up the fluted details. The real work began when the stone pieces had to be hoisted up the scaffolding as the column began to grow over the men's heads.

"I'M REALLY SORRY this happened Aubrey," Samantha said softly. "You know, we're kind of alike these days. I live at Hydrangea Hall now, and you're working at Fairview. We both have these enormous houses in our lives." Samantha watched for a reaction in Aubrey's face. Nothing. She softly rubbed her fingertips over the top of Aubrey's hand as she held it.

Nothing.

"My move was tough, but I have new friends now. They helped me find out all this cool stuff about Hydrangea Hall." Samantha's mind searched for things to talk about to someone who wasn't holding up her end of the conversation.

"Oh!" she suddenly remembered. "Our houses are

related!" Samantha squeezed Aubrey's hand a little harder. "Well not really *related*, but this is so cool, Aubrey! There was a man at your Fairview who was a taxidermist. Oh, I wish you could talk to me, Aubrey. I thought it was so neat when I found it! I think his name was Brightman. No Brighton, I think it was. He studied under the second husband of the woman who owned my Hydrangea Hall – Mr. Wells!" Aubrey's eyelids flicked ever so slightly.

"Oh Aubrey!" Samantha tried to keep her excited voice quiet. "Maybe you think it's neat, too! Mr. Wells was a naturalist, like Darwin. Maybe you know that. And Darwin was a taxidermist, too. I read that all those naturalists kind of had to be, back then." Samantha thought she saw another flicker under Aubrey's lids.

"Mr. Brighton, if I have that name right, was a naturalist and a very famous taxidermist. He studied with Mr. Wells in Rochester. Mr. Brighton even came up with his own formula for preserving the skins. His taxidermy still looks great because no bugs get into his specimens because of the arsenic he used."

Aubrey's eyes fluttered incessantly, her eyes even flying open for a second.

"Oh! Aubrey!" Samantha shouted over her shoulder toward the hallway while trying to keep her eyes on Aubrey. "Aunt Lenora! Aunt Lenora!"

Aubrey's mother flew into the room without a gown. Mr. and Mrs. Whitaker clogged the doorway, and a nurse pushed her way through.

"What's wrong, Samantha?"

"She opened her eyes, Aunt Lenora! Only for a second, but Aubrey opened her eyes!"

The nurse politely shoved past them, swiftly and efficiently checking Aubrey's tubes and vitals.

"There was a spike in her vitals, but nothing to be worried about, Mrs. Harrison. These things happen. I wouldn't worry."

The nurse worked silently for a few more minutes at a small computer station while the family looked on in anticipation. Then the nurse left them staring at Aubrey as the machines breathed for her.

"I know she opened her eyes, Aunt Lenora," Samantha said quietly. "I know she did."

"I believe you, Sam," she said.

Thirty-eight

WARREN HAD been missed. After a brief and tolerable reprimand by the supervisor Hadaway had left in charge, Warren was sent with a group of men to work on the new garden temple. Warren and the three men he was working with had just hoisted their piece of the column into place. Another was already secured with ropes and leather bindings. The men had slung a rope over a large branch of a nearby oak to haul the column piece into the air. Men on the scaffolding were ready to catch it and set it into place. The men then climbed around to adjust the scaffolding while the crew on the ground secured the next piece of the column. It was growing rapidly along with the tenor of the men's grunting and moaning. It had been a long day, and the last piece, now swinging into place, would raise the column to its full twelve-foot height. Warren stood with his hands on his hips watching the men above him ease it into place as much with their skill as with their shouts and curses.

The pieces had to be balanced perfectly. The five columns, each four feet in diameter, would support a massive stone dome, ready and waiting to be lifted into place by a team of horses hitched to ropes and pulleys. The garden temple, hidden in the woods, would provide new, more appropriate shade for the white marble statue of Diana the Huntress.

What happened next was one of the mysteries of Fairview. Some of the crew eventually blamed the incident on exhaustion. Others remembered the bizarre burst of weather as the dried leaves and twigs rose up from the ground in a dizzying twist of wind that drew the surrounding trees into a frenzied dance.

But from where she stood among the trees, Aubrey knew better. At the center of the whirlwind was Maeve in all her ferocity. "I hate you! I hate you!" she cried as she flew at the newly set column, arms outstretched, striking it with all the force of the underworld.

"No, Maeve! No! You don't mean it!" Aubrey screamed.

For a moment the column seemed to teeter with indecision, but it was too late. The men on the scaffolding clamored for safe footing as the scaffolding gave way beside the falling stone pieces. And the men on the ground, Warren among them, abruptly shifted their attention toward Aubrey's shouts and where she stood among the trees, instead of toward the impending danger. Warren turned his eyes skyward just as the pieces of stone fell like comets from the heavens.

"Noooooo!" Aubrey's voice trailed away with the freak wind.

Maeve rose triumphant into the air, evil satisfaction in her smile.

Warren rose too, or a translucent version of him. He rose, his face confused and imploring. He reached one hand toward Maeve, and the satisfaction slid from her face. And as Warren reached out his hand, his body seemed pulled away from the glen, into the trees, and he disappeared.

Thirty-nine

SOMEWHERE, someone screamed.

Aubrey never saw it happen. She had instinctively covered her face with her hands. When she removed them, the ache in the back of her throat told her the scream had been hers. The scene under the trees resembled a battle zone. A cacophony of shouting voices of the living, the moaning of the injured, the silence of the dead. She fell onto the ground in a heap and wept.

But an image of Maeve, her brows drawn together in a fragile bewilderment, rose in front of Aubrey and bade her raise her head. Through tears that ran down her cheeks in rivers, Aubrey glared at the apparition that hovered above her.

"Damn you!" Aubrey hollered, choking on her tears. "How could you?"

"He deserved it," Maeve reasoned, but her wavering voice sounded unconvinced. "An eye for an eye."

"You don't know. You don't!" Aubrey was drowning in her spit and tears as she wept.

"I do know!" Maeve said, her voice stubbornly self-righteous. "He murdered me!"

"I don't know what?" It wasn't Maeve, but a man who spoke as he placed a caring hand on her shoulder. It was Dalton. But questions spilled out as he bent to help her up and lifted his eyes to survey the scene at that same time. "Oh God, Aubrey! What are you doing here? What has happened?" Aubrey's vision was still so clouded with Maeve's proclamation, she barely noticed Dalton.

The apparition moved back slightly, watching her. Although Dalton worked to support her, Aubrey's hands sought out a nearby tree trunk, her fingers dug into the ruts of its bark. She hauled herself to her feet with what must have been an inhuman strength because she had nothing left. Aubrey wanted to holler, but she was spent. "No!" It came out quiet, adamantly.

"No, what Aubrey? Really, we must get you away from here. This is no place for a lady." He looked back over his shoulder at the destruction as he led Aubrey toward Fairview. The scene kept replaying in her head like one of those old black and white movies stuck in the projector. And, at one point, when they were easing up the walkway through the blue and white garden, Aubrey had to stop, doubling over and covering her mouth for fear she would vomit at the site of Warren in her mind's eye.

"No," she repeated in a quiet utterance Dalton took as regret.

How he got her onto the sofa in the salon was beyond her. She was still sobbing, the silent, shoulder-shaking sobbing when a world is ending. She shook her head as Dalton, who now knelt before her, offered her a glass of water that had appeared from nowhere. She dried her eyes with the back of her hand.

"My God, what happened here?" Claire appeared at the commotion.

"Not here, Claire. In the glen." He offered Aubrey his handkerchief. "An accident. A horrible, horrible accident."

"Not another one."

He lowered his head, and when he spoke again, his voice was uncomprehending. "The columns the men were building fell." Claire sat down next to Aubrey. "Looks like the pieces crushed one of the workers," he added quietly. "There are others hurt, too."

Claire gasped. "I should go." She made to leave.

"No, Claire. It's no place for ladies. The men seemed to have it…" he realized how unfeeling he was going to sound. "…under control. They'll come to you when they need you." He turned his attention back to Aubrey. "What were you doing there, dear girl?" he prodded patiently, taking the glass of water from her shaking hands. "Did you see the accident?"

She looked into his face, and her eyes began to fill with tears, but he could not possibly understand their magnitude. Everything had come crashing down.

"Of course you did." He stood and walked to the fireplace and, resting his hand on the mantle, stared into the vacant space.

How would she explain it to them? What parts did they even care about? What parts would they believe? Had Maeve just died again? Had that only been moments ago? No, no, it couldn't have been. Claire and Dalton were too calm for her death just to have happened. And she was back with them, not just watching them. There must have been another jump in time. Scenarios flowed like ribbons through her brain intertwining, spinning and swirling. She had to figure this out. She buried her head in her hands pulling on her hair. She focused on Dalton standing at the fireplace staring at the white stuffed peacock on the mantelpiece. Dalton, running his hand soothingly down the back of the beautiful white bird.

There was her answer.

It stood before her like another apparition, yet perfectly clear to her. The pieces had all fallen into place, some as distant as Mrs. Davidson's science class and Aubrey's curious probing into the Periodic Table of Elements that Mrs. Davidson had given to her students.

She raised her head and took in Dalton's mustachioed, sad-eyed countenance, then Claire's visage, who, for the first time since Aubrey had arrived, truly looked concerned about her. Claire placed her hand supportively over Aubrey's.

"You don't have to talk about it if you don't want to, dear," Claire soothed. "But sometimes it helps."

It was the kind of thing Aubrey's mother would have said. For the slightest moment, Aubrey wondered if she would ever see her mother again, but she pushed the thought aside.

"I know how Maeve died," Aubrey said cautiously.

Claire put a hand to her throat and felt the pearls there. "The doctor said it was her heart."

"I don't think so," Aubrey said. "She had probably been feeling sick for weeks, her stomach."

"Well, yes –"

"Just a summer bug," Dalton said, his attention drawn to the new conversation. "You can't die from that."

"No," Aubrey said. "But you can die from arsenic poisoning."

"Arsenic? Poisoning?" Claire stood as her voice rose in disbelief. "Who would be poisoning my daughter?"

"I don't think it was done on purpose, Mrs. Somerton," Aubrey continued. "Maeve was poisoning herself."

"Poisoning herself?" Claire cut in. "Why would she do that?" She collapsed onto the sofa again, covering her face. "No! Not because I wanted her to marry Frank! No, no! We would have been able to find another way."

"No, no, Mrs. Somerton." It was Aubrey who now took Claire's hand. "I think it was inadvertent."

"This is quite a theory you are weaving." Dalton settled himself at the edge of a chair.

"It is a theory," Aubrey admitted. "But it rings true. Maeve's death was just another – unfortunate accident." She had their attention now. "You see, the animals." Aubrey looked toward the bird that Dalton had just been petting. "Maeve loved them. Especially Bertie, when he died."

"There's been too much death here," Claire looked away. "Even the damned bird."

Dalton raised his eyebrows in surprise at the crack in Claire's veneer.

"I'm sorry," she apologized.

"It's all right, Mrs. Somerton. Do you remember Maeve petting the animals as if they were alive?"

"Yes. Yes, you're right. She did love them. She called them her zoo."

"Well, Mr. Brighton had concocted a recipe all his own for preserving the animals. He taught it to your husband, and he used it too. You can ask Mr. Brighton about it if you don't believe me. But the mixture he painted on the inside of the skins to preserve them and keep bugs away contained a lot of arsenic. Mr. Brighton used gloves in the process, and taught your husband to use gloves as well. Everyone else here uses gloves to handle the taxidermy, but Maeve didn't. And she touched them more often than she should have. I think the arsenic got on her hands. It either got into her system that way or got onto food she ate because it was on her hands. No one really noticed how much attention Maeve paid to the animals – a little here, a little there – but over time, it all added up."

"I thought it was just to keep them clean," Dalton muttered quietly as he wiped his hands on his trousers.

"How do you know all of this, child?" Mrs. Somerton asked.

"I – I don't know," Aubrey said. "All the pieces just came together. I know you needed to know. And Maeve needed to know."

Claire and Dalton looked at each other with confusion.

Then Aubrey's eyes fluttered, and she faded before them.

"GERARD?" IDA CALLED to him as he passed by in the hall of Fairview.

"Yes?" He backed up and poked his head into the library.

"I seem to have found another sketchbook belonging to Maeve Somerton."

"Really?" Gerard walked over to where she stood near the floor-to-ceiling shelves.

"I swear I have gone through these shelves a million times, Gerard. I don't know how I missed this one." The older woman pushed a lock of grey hair from her eyes, smoothed it into place and tapped the bottom of her bob into shape. She handed it to him. "I'm sure it's hers. Who else's could it be?"

He flipped through, stopping now and again to more closely inspect a drawing.

"You're right. Who else's could it be…and yet, it doesn't quite look like the rest of her sketches. Maybe it's a later one, and she was just getting better."

"Hmm…perhaps." She watched him as he studied the drawings. "I've been thinking. Do you think we should frame a few and hang them somewhere, make a display of them?"

"We could make color copies and hang those. I'm not sure the board of directors would be keen about hanging the originals."

"True – wait, what was that you just passed?"

Gerard turned back a page. "This?"

"Why Gerard." The old woman's eyes widened. She smiled conspiratorially. "I believe that's you!"

"What?" He laid the sketchbook open on the nearby desk so they could both have a good look. It was a sketch of a young man in work clothes. He was sitting on a lawn, his outstretched legs crossed casually at the ankles. He was leaning back on one elbow, the sleeves of his work shirt rolled up to his forearms. His cap was tossed on the ground beside him. He had captivating hazel eyes and curly blond hair framing his face.

"Sure, it could be! Since you've let your hair grow a little longer and since you've – well, since you've started working out –"

Gerard blushed a little realizing that the old woman had noticed. "But how could it be?"

"Well, darned if I know, but if you dressed in those period clothes, that could be you!"

Forty

WHEN AUBREY opened her eyes, her mother was holding her hand.

"Oh my God." The whisper floated to her brain. "It's a miracle."

A nurse appeared, alerted by a beeping machine somewhere nearby. She maneuvered around to the other side of the bed, poked buttons on a monitor, and turned to Aubrey, placing a hand gently on her forehead. "Welcome back, hon," the nurse said to Aubrey. "I'll go get the doctor," she said to Lenora. "Let's see if we can get her off some of this machinery."

Within three days of awakening, Aubrey had made such progress that she was being transferred to a private room in a general medical unit. An attendant rolled her bed off the patient elevator, down a moss-green hallway with brown doors and into a room with a view of the sky, a private bathroom, and a television hanging on the wall. Her mom, who was waiting for her in a chair by a desk, smiled expectantly as she was rolled in. And when the bed was parked into place, Aubrey's heart jumped. A young man stood in the corner smiling shyly.

"Warren!" Aubrey uttered it in a burst of breathless relief.

Concern registered on Lenora's face, but the young man fielded the mistake. He chuckled self-consciously.

"You've only met me once. And more than six weeks ago," he said, cautiously approaching her bed. "My name is Gerard."

Aubrey's face crumbled with bewilderment.

"It's okay, Aubrey." Her mother stood to take her hand. "The doctor said you might be a little confused for a while. Your memory needs a little time to catch up."

She gave a small apologetic smile to her mother and the young man. But it wasn't her memory that was the problem. Except for his modern clothing, he looked just like Warren. Aubrey closed her eyes tight, her brows drawing together in an effort to make her brain function. Pulling the memories into the right time was like trying to right a row boat after it had capsized, all the while treading water beside it.

"It's okay," Gerard said. "I'm the –"

"Yes. I remember you now. I think maybe you look different?"

"Yeah." He gave a light laugh, and patted his non-existent belly. "I'm getting that a lot lately."

"Oh honey, we'll all be a little different! You've lost

more than a month. But we've been with you the whole time. I haven't left, and you're friends – Pitch, Gerard, Ida, – oh, and Aunt Sheila and Uncle Hal and Samantha have been to see you."

"Cool," was all she could think to say about visits she did not remember. She looked back at Gerard, the misperception still confounding her.

"Aubrey, I wanted to make sure you got up here okay, but I really need to get a cup of coffee. I'll be right back, if that's okay, Gerard?" Her mother seemed nervous, and Aubrey wondered why.

"Sure," he said. Aubrey nodded.

Lenora glanced over her shoulder at her daughter as she left the room, a reassurance to herself that her daughter was back.

"So…Gerard," Aubrey started. "You're the guy who was taking me on the tour when –"

"Yeah," he looked down sheepishly. "Look, your mom left because she knew I needed to talk to you. I had to say I was sorry. I've felt horrible about all of this, and I'm really glad you're back."

"I'm sorry I didn't recognize you right away –"

"No, I'm sorry. I've gone over it again and again in my head. I don't know how I could have stopped all this from happening, but I wish I could have." He lowered his eyes. "I'm really glad you're back."

There was an awkward lull in the conversation.

"I'm glad I'm back, too. I hope I'll be better soon, so I get to work at Fairview at least a little this summer. I feel like I know so much more about it now."

"Huh?" It was Gerard's turn to be perplexed.

Aubrey back-peddled as quickly as her mind would let her. "Uh, while I was...well, you know...I had these, like, crazy dreams or something."

"Dreams?"

"Well, I guess." She hesitated, wondering how to frame an experience that now, in the light of day, seemed bizarre. "I was there at Fairview. I got to know Maeve and her mother and her friends."

"That's odd." His words said one thing, but his expression did not seem critical. He pulled over a chair and sat down near her bed.

That expression, and the face that it radiated from, seemed so familiar it gave her the courage to tell him more. "Yeah, it was. I dreamed Maeve thought she had been killed. And for a while, it looked to me like she had been. It wasn't just heart problems, like they think. Her mother had tried to arrange a marriage between her and the landscape designer –"

"Well, that really did happen. We must have mentioned that to you or something, that first day."

"Yeah," she hesitated, knowing they hadn't. "Well," she proceeded cautiously again. "Maeve had fallen in love with a very...charming...worker on the estate." How could she now mention Warren's name without total embarrassment? "I think Hadaway tried to poison Maeve and frame this young man for it in an effort to get him out of the picture, but Maeve was ironically –"

"Poisoning herself? You know, while you were here, we just came across the formula her father was using for the taxidermy, and we couldn't believe the amount of –"

"Arsenic!" she jumped in.

"Yeah, arsenic – Wait. How can you know all of this stuff if you claim it was only a dream?" Gerard wondered out loud.

"Well, you know, my mom is a psychic. Maybe it runs in the family?" she suggested sheepishly.

He chuckled. "Maybe," he said, but something in his eyes told Aubrey he was seriously considering the idea.

There was another awkward lull in the conversation. Then Gerard dug a piece of paper out of his pocket and unfolded it. It was a photo copy of the sketch he and Ida had found several days ago at Fairview.

"Hey, I've been carrying this around for a couple of days, waiting for you to –" He smiled self-consciously. "Anyway, do you recognize this?"

Aubrey took it from him, drew up her knees under the covers, and using her legs as an easel, gently smoothed the creases in the drawing. "Oh, Warren," she said tenderly. She felt her eyes filling, and she hastily batted tears away.

"So this is him?" Gerard inquired.

"Yeah, I drew it."

"What?" Gerard shook his head and smiled at what must be a joke.

"I mean Maeve drew it," Aubrey covered.

Gerard pressed on rather than try to make sense of the comment. She must have been kidding. "The sketchbook that this picture came from, Ida just found it in the library. Says she knows every book in that room and has never, ever seen this one before."

Aubrey reluctantly handed the drawing of Warren back to Gerard.

When he took the drawing back from her, he noticed a tiny $\mathcal{AH}$ written in the corner. Why hadn't he and Ida noticed this before? This was not Maeve's drawing, he realized, and his head swam at the possibilities.

"So…" Gerard said trying to fill the void left while the gears in his mind cranked into overdrive. "All this time, we've thought Maeve died of a heart attack, but it was a death that could have been prevented?"

"Had people understood at the time, I suppose so."

"Do you think Maeve would be happy with this conclusion?"

"Maeve?" She was shocked at the conspiratorial look he was giving her. "I don't know," she said slowly, quietly. "She was a complicated person. She wouldn't have been satisfied, no. But a piece of her would have found solace in knowing she hadn't been murdered. She was just sad she had died so young."

She looked up wondering if Gerard would think her insane. He nodded in thoughtful agreement.

"Well," he said, lightly slapping the bed next to her legs. "When you get sprung from this joint, how about we spend a day at Awagashat Lake? Have a picnic? Or if your physical therapist feels you can handle it, a bike ride?"

Aubrey smiled. This was her Warren back. "Sure."

"Good." He stood to leave. "I've got to go pull my shift at Fairview. Here," he handed her back the drawing.

"You keep this. The initials in the corner are weirding me out."

Aubrey eyes filled with tears of relief.

"I'll see you soon," he said as he paused at the door. There was something about her. He had felt it from the very first time he had seen her. And he would make sure they had time now to figure out exactly what the connection was – no matter how peculiar.

"Gerard?"

He answered "yes" with his eyes.

"Could you make sure Bertie gets put somewhere special? Not in that alcove off to the side." Aubrey's face wrinkled in concentration.

"The parlor mantle?"

"Yes!" Her eyes brightened. "That would be good. Gerard –" she added as an afterthought, "remember to wear gloves."

"Definitely." He chuckled and turned to leave.

"You know, Gerard –" He turned back to look at her. "Even if we could have seen into the future, we wouldn't have had the power to change any of it."

"I know," he said. "But we can make sure things are good from now on."

Author's Notes

THERE ARE THOSE who believe that there is only so much energy in the world. When a person dies, their soul is reborn near those who have loved it the most, so that as living beings, we are continually surrounded by those who have left us. It is why, inexplicably, we are drawn to certain people. Simply put, we have known them before.

I have always thought this to be an intriguing theory, and so it is the basis for *Eye of the Peacock*. What would happen, I wondered, if a person could go back in time and meet the people who surrounded them now? And so, the idea of sending Aubrey back in time took seed.

In the process of writing this novel, a few of my beta readers wanted to tie Warren and Gerard more closely to each other. Surely, they must be related – Gerard the great-great-grandson of Warren – or something like that. But I challenge my readers to embrace the more supernatural connection – that of Aubrey and Gerard – who find each other through time and place. It is only a bud of a relationship, but surely, it has the blessings of Time.

The story's setting also transcends time. Several years ago, my family and I visited a beautiful estate in the picturesque Finger Lakes Region of New York State, Sonnenberg – or "Sunny Hill." The home and surrounding 50-acre grounds, built by Frederick and Mary Clark Thompson, are nothing short of magnificent. After her husband's death in 1889, Mrs. Thompson made sure the property fulfilled her husband's dream. As she mourned, Mary travelled through Europe and Asia. It was during those travels that she was inspired by the gardens she saw. When she came home, she expanded her ideas for elaborate gardens, accented by statuary she had purchased abroad. She also became a beloved philanthropist in the area. In my imagination, during our tour, Sonnenberg Gardens in Canandaigua, New York, became the inspiration for Fairview.

While touring the estate, it was noted that the Thompsons remained childless. I was left wondering what it would have been like for a child to grow up there, as I thought the gardens were a wonderful playground. So, I allowed Maeve to grow up on a similar estate. Mary Clark Thompson did have a sister, who visited often with her children, and so I allowed Claire to have a sister as well, mostly so that the readers could see Claire in an atmosphere of sibling joy.

For those of you who have read my first novel, *Relic*,

the two estates that inspired the settings truly are connected, as Samantha tells Aubrey. In *Relic*, Hydrangea Hall was inspired by Hillside in Wyoming, New York. The woman who owed that estate was Lydia Avery Coonley Ward. Her second husband, Henry Augustus Ward, was a famous naturalist and geologist. In *Eye of the Peacock*, Mr. Brighton, who preserved Maeve's beloved Bertie, was modeled loosely after William Temple Hornaday, who assisted Mary Clark Thompson with her aviary collection. Turns out that Henry Ward and William Hornaday knew each other. After attending college, Hornaday went to work for Ward's National Science Foundation in Rochester, New York. So, in an odd way, the two homes are connected.

Sonnenberg Gardens is a New York State park open to the public and kept operational through donations and a vast collection of devoted volunteers. As a non-profit organization, they are responsible for their own operating costs. I encourage you to visit. See the glory of the inspiration for yourself. Experience the surprises around every corner, and get a taste of the wonderful life Maeve was so sorry to leave behind.

Acknowledgements

MY SINCEREST thanks to all of the wonderful people at Sonnenberg Gardens, from the docents, who didn't know I was in their tour groups, to people in the gift shop, who helped me find background information, to the administrators who answered my requests for information, so that I could keep *Eye of the Peacock* true to the time period. You are a wonderfully dedicated group of people protecting a living history that is irreplaceable.

Continued thanks to the ever-encouraging members of the Ken-Ton Writer's Group. Your interest in and critique of my efforts continue to push me forward – and often-times make for quite interesting internal conversations on my way home. A special thank you to my Beta Readers: Amelia Waddell, Elizabeth La Porta and Sean Scarisbrick, whose honesty and sometimes cryptic margin notes – once decoded – had a major influence on this project's final form. Amelia, I hope you are happier with Pitch; Liz, I hope Daisy is safer in your eyes; and Sean, I hope you are pleased with Samantha's cameo. Thanks also go out to Patricia Smith, Elizabeth La Porta, Marsha Sullivan, Jim Worthington and Charlotte Worthington, who kept their eyes on the small details for me. I once again thank my cover designer Aaron La Porta, whose wonderful skill in graphic design has captured the mood and my sometimes elusive ideas for my story.

And my loving thank you to Jim, Charlotte and Clara for allowing me the time and space I need to follow my dream.

About the Author

ROBERTA WORTHINGTON holds a bachelor's degree in print journalism, a bachelor's degree in secondary English education, and a master's degree as a reading specialist. She has been telling stories for as long as she can remember, sometimes others' while working as a newspaper reporter, and often her own to entertain her English students. *Eye of the Peacock* is her second novel.

Roberta resides in Western New York with her husband and their two daughters. Please visit htttp://RobertaWorthington.blogspot.com to learn more.

Also by Roberta Worthington

"I heard someone say once that Fate throws people together because they need each other. Maybe that was why she was drawn to me. Maybe she sensed a kindred spirit."

For twelve-year-old Samantha Whitaker, her parents' dream of running a country inn, which she calls "the Ick," is pure torture.

After purchasing a strange item in an antique shop just to annoy her mother, Samantha makes a desperate attempt to flee the small village by stealing her parents' car – only to crash it when an odd village girl darts in front of her…then disappears.

An unusual relic, a hidden diary, an unfinished letter. Will Samantha's supernatural sleuthing bring answers to a village mystery that has strange parallels to her own life?

Available at Amazon.com